BE MY BOO

A SWEETLY SPOOKY HALLOWEEN ROMANCE
NOVELLA

MISHA CREWS

FREE STORY

Just for you: a free copy of my fun holiday short story *All I Want for Christmas is a Happy Halloween.* Just go to mishacrews.com/freebook, or click the image in your ebook to start reading!

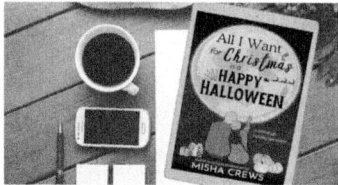

DEAR READER,

Well, first let me say, Happy Halloween! This is the first book I've written which is set on Halloween night, and it is inspired by my love of autumn, as well as my fondness for haunted house stories.

Boo is different from most of the books and stories that I've written, but it does have several elements that are found in most of my work: a cute romantic couple, a big house full of secrets, and the complexities of family relations (both blood-related and found family).

So, even though this is a departure from my usual fare—more on how it came about in the Author's Note at the end—I hope you find it a fun Halloween frolic.

I'll see you at the end of the book!

Hugs and happy reading,

Misha

PROLOGUE

Anyone with half a brain could tell that Wicklow House was haunted. Then again, who doesn't love a haunted house on Halloween?

I mean, sure, the place was beautiful. It had been built of gray stone, which glinted silver in the moonlight, and the lines of the many-gabled roof still stood sharp and true against the sky. Roses even bloomed occasionally in the summer garden.

But for all of that, the old mansion was a blight on the landscape. Crumbling and broody, its thick walls seemed to turn a cold shoulder to the world at large, while its windows glared at those who dared to pass by.

The house had been empty for as long as anyone in the nearby town of Wickdale could remember. Those who crossed the threshold claimed to hear strange noises. Footsteps in empty rooms, whispers where no one stood, various moans and groans. You know the drill. The house kept its secrets locked up tight, almost as if waiting for the perfect person to wander in, trip over a ghost or two, and make things interesting.

That's where our hero comes in. Dale Carpenter, stout of heart and square of jaw. You'll get to know him better later. There's also a girl involved, of course. And there's even a dog, if you can believe it. Honestly, the whole scenario is a little bit "Scooby-Doo-meets-rom-com."

On the other hand, Fred and Daphne never had to face anything like what happened to our hero and heroine on the sinister night when this Halloween tale takes place.

I wish I could tell you, Dear Reader, that everything works out okay. But all I can do is promise to be with you every step of the way. Just think of me as your humble storyteller, your guide along the candle-lit pathway of this haunted Halloween romance.

Oh, and I'm also the ghost.

Boo!

CHAPTER
ONE

Dale

Dale's first thought on entering the town of Wickdale was that it must have been designed with Halloween in mind. Pretty little houses, lined up along quiet streets, were fronted by maple trees that flamed fiery red and gold. Pumpkins adorned every doorstep, cobwebs stretched across windows, and ghostly decorations hung from porch railings.

Dale brought his pickup truck to a slow stop in front of the town hall, where cornstalks flanked the double doors. Across the street, in the village square, the townsfolk had embraced the season with an enthusiasm that bordered on the theatrical. Strings of orange and purple lights twinkled from lampposts, casting an eerie glow over the cobblestone paths that led from the sidewalk to an old-fashioned pavilion.

Next to the pavilion, a towering scarecrow stood guard, surrounded by hay bales and cornstalks. Although there was still one night to go before Halloween, the festivities had already begun. Costumed vendors ladled cider and handed out treats as children darted amongst the spooky decorations. Even the stone steps of the town hall held hand-carved jack-o'-lanterns, which flickered with candlelight.

"Wow," Dale said. "I hope those aren't real candles."

His best friend, Jenner, who was riding shotgun, barked out a laugh. "You're all business, aren't you, buddy?"

Dale shifted, wishing he felt as free as Jenner to join in the good humor of the evening. "That's why we're here, isn't it?" he asked defensively.

"Well, yeah, but you don't have to play Fire Marshall Bill every second of every day, do you?"

The truck was still idling. Jenner reached over from the passenger seat and turned the ignition off. "Seriously, man, I'm glad you could come with me on this job. Wouldn't be the same without you. I know that this is a difficult time of year."

Dale frowned. The words were kindly meant, but he rarely thought about his past, and never talked about it. Never.

Jenner, knowing that he wouldn't get a response, reached for the door handle. "Come on, let's go meet the mayor. If I remember right from the town's website, she's kind of a hottie."

Dale couldn't help but chuckle. On the job, Jenner was a heck of a firefighter, and there was nobody else

Dale would want beside him when the smoke got thick. Off the job, Jenner had a one-track mind—*women*—and no regulator. But he was harmless.

Dale pocketed his keys and hustled to follow Jenner into the town hall. He found his partner inside, talking to a woman in a business suit. She was, indeed, very attractive, with dark hair and a slim figure.

"—avoid the same situation from happening again," she was saying.

"Absolutely," Jenner agreed. "That's what we're here for."

He caught sight of Dale. "Oh good, here's my partner."

He made a quick introduction between Dale and Mayor Rosaleigh

Tanji, who extended a hand for him to shake.

"Pleased to meet you," she said. "I'm very glad that you two are available to help us this year."

"Of course," Dale said. "It's our pleasure. Fire prevention is as much our job as fire fighting."

"The mayor was just telling me that they've had a couple of incidents in the past two weeks." Jenner crossed his arms. The sincere expression was back, and this time it wasn't a put-on. He took his job seriously. "Candles left unattended, that sort of thing."

"Nothing major, thank goodness," Mayor Tanji said. "We have a very good Volunteer Fire Department. But after the second small fire in as many weeks, we need to act. I've scheduled you to visit the elementary and high schools tomorrow so that you can remind everyone about the importance of risk reduction.

We've done this already, of course, but I'm hoping that you'll be taken more seriously than we were."

"Absolutely," Dale agreed. "We're happy to help."

Jenner added, "Dale can also sit in with your VFD tomorrow night, in case they need an extra pair of hands. I would do it myself, but our bosses have asked me to work on some manuals for our new recruits." He gave a self-effacing shrug. "I'm known as something of a writer."

Dale managed to avoid rolling his eyes. Jenner used the writing line when he was trying to sound extra interesting to women. Although, to give the man credit, he was pretty good with words, and he had indeed helped to write training manuals.

Either way, Mayor Tanji appeared unimpressed.

"If we can just make it through the next thirty-six hours without anyone getting hurt, I'll call this a success." Her eyes were distant, dark. "Last year we had the devil of a time keeping kids out of that old, abandoned house down the road."

"Oh boy," Jenner said. "What happened?"

The mayor started to tell her story, but Dale didn't hear it. Because immediately after Jenner had asked his question, the front door opened, and a ghost walked in.

CHAPTER
TWO

Dale

It wasn't a Halloween ghost. There was no sheeted costume or white powder makeup. This ghost looked like a woman that Dale hadn't seen for two decades.

He knew that was ridiculous, of course. For one thing, the woman that Dale knew wasn't dead, so she couldn't be a ghost. And for another thing, ghosts didn't exist.

The woman who had entered appeared to be in her late thirties or early forties. She had a round figure and very good posture. Her hair was thick and blond, and fell straight on each side of her stern, pretty face. She was wearing a tweed coat over a burgundy turtleneck. The coat had a stain near the left pocket. The stain was Dale's fault. When he was a child, he had put some chocolates in that pocket, thinking it would be a treat for later. He hadn't realized they would melt.

But again, he reminded himself, *that is not the same coat, because that is not the same woman, because that's impossible.*

Nevertheless, he couldn't stop himself from speaking as she approached. "Aunt Kell?"

The woman didn't respond. Her hard shoes made slapping sounds as she moved past the three standing in the lobby and continued down a wide corridor behind them.

Dale glanced at his companions. Neither Jenner nor Mayor Tanji appeared to have heard him speak, or reacted to this apparition, if that's what the woman was. His eyes slid back to the figure of the woman, disappearing down the hallway. And before he knew it, he was following.

It was after five o'clock, and the building appeared to be mostly deserted. The hallway lights had been turned off, but illumination came from a distant door, as if someone had left a lamp lit on the desk. That was where the woman was headed.

Dale hadn't seen his aunt Kell since he was eleven. Not only would she have been decades older than the woman he was following down the hallway, but she had also been in a wheelchair for over twenty years. And since Dale was her only living relative, he assumed that he would have been notified if she had died.

Not that it made a difference, right? Because *ghosts didn't exist.*

Ahead of him, the woman turned right into the office with the desk lamp. Dale found himself moving faster, needing to see the woman, needing to speak to her and know for sure—"Aunt Kell?" His voice was a whimper, needy and plaintive.

He reached the doorway, looked inside.

The office was empty.

DALE DOWNED three beers before his hands stopped shaking.

"Whoa, slow down, man." Jenner fiddled with the saltshaker as Dale polished off his third bottle and signaled the waitress for one more. "I know it's kind of party time around here, but we've got to work tomorrow."

Dale's pulse finally slowed from a full-on sprint to a leisurely stroll. The alcohol was working its magic, spreading warmth through every icy part of him.

"You're right." He got the waitress's attention again and waved a hand to cancel the next bottle. She nodded in reply.

They were at the local tavern, which was hopping for the middle of the week. Here, too, Halloween had made itself known. There was orange beer on tap, paper bats hanging from the ceiling, and battery-operated plastic pumpkins on the table. A skeleton by the door laughed every time someone new walked over the threshold.

Dale turned his attention to the plate of food in front of him, a giant burger and fries which had arrived with his last drink. He had to hold the burger with both hands and open his mouth all the way to take a bite.

The food was already cooling, but the heavy smoky flavor was comforting, and the protein was invigorating.

As he chewed, his mind cleared, and he tuned in to what Jenner was saying.

"So, I'm rethinking my plans for tomorrow night. One of us should keep an eye on that house."

"What house?" Dale asked.

"Dude. What have I been talking about for the last twenty minutes?" Jenner frowned. "Are you sure you're okay?"

The question was irritating.

"Of course I'm okay. Am I supposed to pay attention every time you speak?" Dale popped a fry into his mouth and chomped, feigning nonchalance. "Ninety percent of what you say is weapons-grade baloney. Knowing you, this could be an outhouse we're talking about. Is it an outhouse?"

That elicited a laugh. "I'm talking about Wicklow House. Old abandoned place outside of town that's supposed to be haunted."

Dale's throat closed at Jenner's words, sticking the French fry in his throat. He reached for his beer, remembered it was empty, and picked up his water instead. He swallowed painfully and forced himself to speak.

"Haunted, sure. We should be really worried about that."

"Kids like to break in there, and one of them might get hurt."

Jenner took a swig of his own beverage, and Dale

noticed for the first time that his friend was drinking ginger ale. Hm. The only reason Jenner would have chosen a soft drink over a beer was if he thought there might actually be some emergency rescuing to do.

"So," Jenner went on, "Not only is Rosaleigh concerned about teeny-boppers burning down their houses because they're lighting candles while they listen to Alice Cooper records, or whatever kids do these days—"

"You're thirty-two," Dale reminded him. "Alice Cooper was at least a generation before you. Two or three generations before these kids."

"Not only is she concerned about that," Jenner continued forcefully, "she's also worried that some-one's going to get themselves killed clowning around in a haunted house. The town even went so far as to have the place inspected, in case it needed to be condemned. It's in good shape, apparently, from the floors to the flues, but that doesn't mean it's a safe place for a Halloween shindig."

Dale forced himself to ignore his friend's use of the word "shindig," and asked, "Can't the police keep an eye on it?"

"There are three cops in this town. They can't spare one to sit at that house all night."

"So, what do you want to do? Play security guard? I thought you were going to be 'writing' tomorrow, while I hang with the local Volunteer Fire Department."

Jenner waved his hand. "This is obviously more important than trying to make time with Mayor

Gorgeous. I'll camp out at the old house tomorrow night, and you can be on duty with the VFD."

Dale glowered. "Why do I have to be on duty while you get to rack out?"

"It's not racking out, my friend. It's guard duty. On alert, all night long. Scaring away teenagers, investigating strange noises, fighting off stray racoons. That kind of thing." Jenner took another sip of ginger ale. "You don't need that stress."

Dale had picked up another French fry, but he tossed it back on the pile. "You don't think I can handle a night in an empty house?"

"Come on, brother." Jenner looked uncomfortable. "I know you can handle it, I just figure…"

"What? That I'll flip out?" Dale felt his anxiety start to climb again. His temper kicked in right along with it. "You think you'll find me rocking back and forth in a corner somewhere?"

Jenner pushed his plate away. "Look, there's a reason that you don't usually work on October thirty-first, right? Truth is, I wouldn't have even asked you to come here except that Freddy came down with the flu."

"Wow, thanks for that. Good to know I have your confidence."

"You do have my confidence—"

"Then let me take guard duty, and you hang with the VFD."

"—but I also know you very well," Jenner persisted. "And I'm technically senior, here, so I'm making the work assignments."

Dale stared at his plate of congealing food. The

half-burger and fries that he had already consumed sat uncomfortably in his stomach. He tried to remember the last meal he'd eaten with his family, but he couldn't. That final day was a blur. Except for the weeping.

Tears threatened, and he blinked them away.

Suddenly, he dug angrily into the pocket of his jeans. He found a quarter, pulled it out, and slapped it onto the table with a force that made his palm sting.

"Flip me for it."

Jenner buckled his lower lip and shook his head slowly. "I'm not going to flip you for it."

Dale leaned forward. "Flip me for it, or I quit."

Jenner huffed a half-laugh as he picked up his drink. "Stubborn son of a gun."

"You better believe it." Dale pushed his own plate aside and slid the quarter into the open space between himself and Jenner. "Flip."

THREE

Dale

And that was how Dale ended up in a haunted house on Halloween night.

He woke up that morning with a mild headache that he vanquished with two cups of coffee and forty minutes on the hotel treadmill. As he showered afterward, he told himself he had made the right decision about staying in the house that night.

Dale was a grown man. He was a firefighter who pulled people from burning buildings. And he was not afraid of ghosts, because ghosts did not exist.

Halloween celebrations, however, *did* exist, and it was surprisingly refreshing to tour the local schools with Jenner, and see the decorations, costumes, and general air of excitement that shone over all the day's activities. Was there anything in life as fun as being a kid on Halloween?

Despite the general mood of revelry, the kids that he and Jenner addressed were responsive, even the teenagers. Dale had the satisfaction of feeling that his words made a difference. Of course, he hadn't forgotten the woman he thought he'd seen the night before, and everywhere they went, Dale kept his eyes open for her. The smallest glimpse would have been welcome, would have reassured him that he hadn't been imagining things. But he had no luck.

In the early evening, he dropped Jenner off at the VFD. They parted with their customary exchange of affectionate abuses.

Dale: "Don't forget how to use the pole."

Jenner: "Don't forget which end is up."

But before Jenner shut the door, he put his hand on the truck and leaned down to fix Dale with a serious gaze. "Dale…"

"I know." Dale nodded. "It's okay. I got this."

He put the truck in gear. "See you in the morning."

"Yeah. See you in the morning." Jenner smacked the cab in a farewell gesture.

IN TRUE HAUNTED HOUSE STYLE, Wicklow House was located on a back road, in the middle of a barren field. As Dale approached down the one-lane road, details emerged through the gathering gloom. He made out a tall iron gate, gray stone walls and steeply pitched roof. The gate was padlocked, but the mayor had provided a key. Dale unlocked the gateway, drove his truck through, and locked it again behind him.

He had decided to write off last night's "sighting" as a case of tired eyes and mistaken identity. The woman hadn't responded to him because he had called her by someone else's name. She hadn't turned into the empty office, but had gone off in another direction, and Dale hadn't seen it in the darkened hallway. Those were the logical conclusions to the situation.

But as he drove onward toward the house, he wondered. If those conclusions were so logical, why hadn't he asked Jenner or the mayor if they had seen the woman? There had been plenty of opportunities that day for just such a question. It certainly could *not* have been because he didn't want to find out that they had not seen what he had. Right?

He watched the house grow larger and larger in front of him until it blocked out the surrounding countryside entirely. He set the brake and turned his head so he could take in the entire structure. The dark windows which gazed grimly down on him were a strange contrast to the wide, welcoming front porch, with its shallow timeworn steps.

"Oh great," he said. "It's Dracula's Castle meets *The Waltons.*"

He got out of the truck and stood for a long moment, keys in one hand, flashlight in the other. Then he took the plunge. He rounded the truck, climbed the steps, and unlocked the heavy front door. He wanted to see the inside before he unloaded his gear.

One thing about being a fireman, Dale had a good feel for buildings. And from the moment he crossed the threshold, instinct told him that the structure was solid and safe. The front door hung square and swung easily. The floor did not creak as he stepped inside. The place didn't even smell damp. Unearthly terrors notwithstanding, it seemed a safe place to spend the night.

He clicked on his flashlight and moved in an arc, surveying the foyer. The floor was tiled with tiny mosaic pieces in a pattern he recognized but couldn't name. The staircase was a grand sweep of wood, with a runner of ancient purple carpet. Portraits of grumpy-looking people lined the curving wall of the staircase. At the top was a balustrade and a gallery, from which someone could look down and see who was coming and going through the front door.

Dale gave a faint smile. A Hollywood designer couldn't have made it any better.

His spirits rose abruptly. Sure, this was a weird time of year for him, and he was in a weirder situation than he ever would have predicted. But the house had been inspected, and it seemed fine. He had a cooler full of food and two seasons of *The Office* downloaded on his iPad, with an extra battery in case he needed it. If either teenagers or ghosts showed up, maybe they'd have a picnic and watch some TV together.

Whistling, Dale grabbed his backpack, sleeping bag and cooler from the truck. He locked the car, and when the house door closed behind him, he turned the latch.

Off the foyer, he found a room which held an ornate fireplace and some lumps of furniture under sheets. It looked like a living room to him, but it was probably a sitting room or parlor or something old-fashioned like that. Whatever it was called, it seemed like a good place to set up camp.

It wasn't until he had set everything down that he realized that a fire had been laid in the fireplace.

Huh.

He looked closer. Large logs, smaller logs, and kindling had all been neatly arranged in the grate. It was well set up, exactly how he himself would have done it. On the hearth lay matches in an enamel box, and a tarnished brass tray held newspapers that were gray with age, yet dry and almost fresh.

Huh, again.

The only explanation he could muster was that there was indeed a party planned in the house that night, and the fire was going to be part of the atmosphere. Well, far be it from Dale to look an atmospheric gift-fire in the mouth. He would get it blazing, and when the kids showed up for the festivities, he would send them on their way with a "thank you and goodnight."

He checked the damper. It opened easily, so he rolled up a piece of newspaper, lit it, then used it to prime the flue. When that was done, he uttered a mental *here-goes-nothing* and ignited the fire.

The kindling caught, and soon the logs were blazing away. The crackling warmth brought a measure of cheer to the place, while at the same time increasing the haunted house atmosphere by a factor of twenty. Dale watched the flames for a few moments through the steel fire screen, then decided to unroll his sleeping bag and get comfortable.

He had just reached for his pack when he heard it—
a soft, almost imperceptible sound, like the padding of
small feet on the wooden floor.

Pat-pat.

Then it came again, only faster.

Pat-pat-pat.

Could the place have rats? Dale's stomach roiled at
the thought. If there were rodents in the house, he
would be spending the night in his truck, thank you
very much.

Moving slowly, wanting to surprise the critters
before they had a chance to hide, he picked up his
flashlight and clicked it on. He swept the beam across
the room, ready for beady red eyes or the slide of gray
fur. But there was nothing there.

He rose slowly to his feet and swept the room again.
Nothing. The sound had stopped, and the house had
fallen silent, except for the crackle of the fire.

Dale let out a breath and shook his head, feeling like
an idiot.

"Man up, smoke eater," he grumbled. "You can't be
jumping at every little noise. The night's just getting
started."

He bent down for his bag, and the sound returned.

Pat-pat-pat-pat-pat.

This time, it was followed by a soft growl. Dale
whirled around, his flashlight flickering as the beam
landed on a small, shadowy figure at the edge of the
room. His heart skipped a beat before he realized what
he was looking at.

It was a dog.

CHAPTER
FOUR

Dale

The animal stepped into the light, revealing a scruffy brown and white coat and bright, intelligent eyes. One ear stood upright, while the other flopped lazily. The dog tilted its head, as if sizing Dale up, then padded closer, its tail wagging slightly.

"Hey there, boy." Dale extended a hand. "Where'd you come from?"

The dog sniffed his fingers cautiously before giving them a tentative lick.

"You're friendly," Dale chuckled. "And you're not who I expected to find in here, that's for sure."

He stroked the dog's head gently, and when it didn't flinch or object in any way, he scratched the silky fur behind its ears. There was a jingling sound, and Dale's hand made contact with something that felt like leather.

"Ah, you've got a collar on."

Dale's relief that the animal was not a random stray clashed with a sense of disappointment that the dog had owners. Careless ones, apparently, who let it get out to explore creepy old houses. He navigated closer to the animal and found the still-jingling tag.

He tilted it toward the light, and made out one word: "Boo."

A chill shot through him, so quickly that it made him gasp, then laugh at his own foolishness.

"Really? Your name is Boo?"

He glanced around him. This had to be a joke, right? First the fire, all laid out nice and tidy, then a dog named Boo? Was this more pre-party hijinks on the part of the local teens?

"Okay 'Boo,' if that is your real name," Dale said. "I guess you're my company for the night, huh? Until someone else shows up."

Of course, the dog chose that moment to twist away from him, and dart through a set of sliding double-doors that led toward the back of the house.

"Hey," Dale protested.

What on earth was going on?

Determined to find out, he rose and followed the dog through the doorway.

He paused just over the threshold, swinging the flashlight to get a sense of his surroundings. Another spacious room with a high ceiling, big pieces of furniture covered with sheets. And books. Shelves upon shelves of books. Apparently, he had just found the library.

What he hadn't found, however, was the dog.

"Boo!" he said sharply, feeling kind of foolish. He still doubted that was the animal's real name.

He walked farther into the room, casting light into shadowy corners. The beam found another fireplace. This one was cold and empty, untouched by human hands. Over the mantle hung a gigantic painting of a very irritated-looking man in a graveyard.

Wait, what?

Dale moved forward and looked closer. The man in the painting was dressed in a cloak and breeches, with boots on his feet. He was indeed standing in a cemetery, with his hand on a headstone. His face was handsome in a long, spare way. But his expression was one of cold hatred, as if he were trying to kill the viewer with his thoughts. He crossed the floor and stood in front of the hearth. The fireplace was huge, nearly six feet high, and probably seven feet wide. Dale knew this because the top of the mantle was about even with his chin.

He looked up, studying the image in the frame. This couldn't be part of the party setup. It would have been too expensive to get such a huge painting made. More than that, Dale doubted that most teenagers would have conceived of something so artsy. So, the guy on the canvas, for all his comical fury, must have been real.

Then Dale caught sight of a brass plate embedded in the frame. It was at eye level, and it read, "J.W. Wicklow, 1868."

Dale moved his flashlight back up to the face. The

painted eyes did that trick where they seemed to look back at him, and Dale could have sworn he felt wrath radiating from the brushstrokes. Whoever the artist had been, he had done a heck of a job.

"J.W. Wicklow, you are one odd duck," Dale said in a low voice. "I don't even want to know why you look so ticked off, sir." He gave an involuntary shudder and tore his gaze away. He knew that it was just a painting, but it was creeping him out, and he didn't want to look at it anymore.

A strange odor came to his nostrils. When he had entered the house it had struck him that the place didn't smell damp. But here, on this spot, not only did it not smell damp, but he also thought he could smell lemons. He closed his eyes and drew a long breath through his nose. Lemons? Really?

Dale opened his eyes and wondered if there was a window open somewhere. That must be it. A window was open, and neighbors were close by, in a house that had been somehow hidden by the landscape.

"And what are they doing?" he asked himself. "Making lemonade with fresh lemons on Halloween night?"

Sure, because that was a thing.

He heard a sound behind him, and turned, expecting to see Boo's eyes glowing in the flashlight. But there was nothing except the humped forms of sheeted furniture. The back of his neck prickled, and he knew Wicklow's image was still staring down at him. He thought of that overused Hollywood phrase, "I sense a presence in the room," and was disgusted with himself for being so emotionally credulous.

Deciding he'd had enough of the library, he moved on to look for Boo elsewhere, determined to at least scope out the first floor before he returned to his mini campsite. He should have done that when he first arrived, anyway. If he hadn't found the dog by the time he was through, he would assume the animal had returned to wherever he'd come from. Maybe he belonged to the lemonade family. Or maybe Dale was just losing his marbles. Who knew?

Dale walked through the kitchen, dining room, and another living-room-slash-sitting-room-slash-parlor. All of them were dark, dusty, and inhabited by ghostly mounds of furniture covered in cloth. Why this stuff hadn't been cleared out or stolen, Dale could not have said.

Back in the foyer, where he could see the glow of the fire from the adjacent room, he paused to examine the mosaic on the floor. The white tiles shone like a full moon, looking pristine against the ebony design. Dale thought he could stare at it for hours. He wondered, briefly, what it would look like from the landing on the second floor.

In the parlor, something went *thump*. Dale's head snapped up, and he held his breath, listening. Except for the very faint sound of crackling flames, all was silent.

Then a shadow passed in front of the fire. Dale saw it very clearly: the light from the fireplace, the brief eclipse of it, then the light again. The shadow was followed by another thump, then the distinctive squeak of his cooler being opened. Someone was in there, and it was definitely not the dog. That cooler had a latch on it that would require opposable thumbs to open. Could it be one of the teenagers?

Dale's first instinct was to call out, to scare away whoever had snuck in and was nosing through his things. But he kept quiet, hoping to catch a glimpse of the intruder. Dale turned off his flashlight and gripped it, club-like, in both hands. He inched forward and stood against the wall that divided the parlor from the foyer, then leaned over and peered around the door.

What he saw was not Boo, or a random teenager, or the ghost of J.W. Wicklow. It was a young woman. She was staring down at his sleeping bag. As he watched, she nudged at it with her toe, then drew back as if expecting something to come slithering out.

Dale glanced around the room. The woman appeared to be alone and didn't exactly look dangerous. She was tallish, curvy, with a cute face and an elfin nose. Her hair was a shade of red that couldn't possibly be real, but it was pretty nonetheless, like maple leaves in autumn.

But what was she doing there?

When she reached for his iPad, he knew the time for looking and thinking was over. He had to act.

"Hey," he said sharply, rounding the corner into the room. "What do you think you're doing?"

The woman shrieked and jumped about a mile into the air. She backed away rapidly as he approached. But she didn't run, and that was something.

"Who are you?" She bit out the words. Her hazel

eyes were wide. "What are you doing here?"

"I could ask you the same thing," he said indignantly. "In fact, I will. Who are you and what are you doing here?"

She crossed her arms. "I asked you first."

"The mayor wanted someone to keep an eye on the place, in case of Halloween partyers."

"Oh." She unfolded her arms and stuffed her hands in the pockets of her sweatshirt. "I'm a photography student. I came to take some pictures for my thesis. I didn't plan to be here so late, but I lost track of time."

Dale nodded slowly. That was a strange explanation, but not impossible. The place was big. There might be a dozen more people in there with them.

The thought gave him the heebie-jeebies, and he was glad to have company—even strange, temporary company.

"I'm Dale Carpenter." He almost held out his hand for her to shake, but didn't want to make any sudden moves in her direction.

She hesitated again, then moved toward him, with her own hand outstretched. "Harmony Lowell," she said.

Dale shook her hand. It was cold but strong, and he released it quickly lest he seemed too creepy. "How long have you been here taking pictures?"

"I got here in the late afternoon," she said. "I wanted to see the place in the magic hour, you know? Long shadows, and all that? But it got dark faster than I expected."

"I didn't see your car out front." The words sounded

a lot more severe than Dale had intended, but they were out of his mouth before he could soften them.

Harmony didn't seem bothered by his tone. She grinned sheepishly. "That's because I parked around back, just in case someone reported a trespasser. Didn't want my boyfriend to have to bail me out of jail. I'm going to be out of here soon, so you'll have the place to yourself. I just have to go grab my camera."

She gestured over her shoulder, indicating the direction of the library. There was an awkward pause, then Harmony turned and drifted out through the double doors.

Dale kept hold of the flashlight and grabbed the electric lantern from his pack before he followed after her. "Oh hey, is that your dog I saw earlier?"

"What dog?"

The young woman's voice drifted to him through the darkness. He lifted the flashlight and watched as she moved directly to the tall bookshelves and started running her fingers along the spines as if looking for a particular book. She didn't seem bothered by the lack of light. Dale wondered if he should have his night vision checked.

Before he could answer her question about the dog, Harmony explained, "When I heard you moving around, I put my camera behind *Tales from Shakespeare* by Charles and Mary Lamb for safekeeping. It was the only book I thought I might remember. Can you believe this whole library is still here?"

"And the furniture, too," Dale agreed. "It's amazing." He leaned against the table, keeping the light focused on the bookshelf in case she needed it. Harmony wasn't beautiful, but she wasn't *not* beautiful, either. Her fingers were quick and nimble as she shifted books around, and her skin shone pale in the flickering firelight. Definitely *not* not-beautiful.

Then Dale noticed something else. He pushed away from the table and stood alert.

"When did you light that fire?" he asked sharply. He distinctly remembered the cold, dark hearth from earlier, underneath the deadly gaze of J.W. Wicklow. Now there was a blaze merrily burning away, filling the room with rosy light.

"What do you mean?" Harmony turned, book in hand. "I thought you lit it."

They looked at each other, then looked back at the fire.

"Is it possible that there's someone else in here with us?" Harmony asked nervously.

"What, like a ghost?"

She shot him a don't-be-ridiculous look. "No, like a real, live person."

"It's a big place," Dale answered slowly. "Are you sure you didn't see anyone when you were here before? Not even the dog?"

"Nobody. And again, *what* dog?"

As if on cue, there was a jingling sound, and toenails clicked on wooden floorboards, announcing the approach of the canine in question. When Boo appeared in the doorway, Harmony cooed with delight and crouched down, holding out her arms and inviting him to be petted.

"He's adorable," she gushed, as Boo happily accepted her invitation. She laughed when she saw the name on his tag. "Why did you name your dog 'Boo'?"

"He's not mine." Dale frowned. "And I take it he's not yours, either."

"I would never let such an adorable creature out of my sight for a minute," she crooned, cupping Boo's face in her hands. "No, I wouldn't."

"Then he's a stray. Or he belongs to someone who's in the house."

She looked up at him with wide, startled eyes. "Do you really think there's someone here?"

"It's not impossible." He explained to her why the mayor had wanted someone in the house, then told her about the fireplace in the other room. "I don't think that whoever is in here is dangerous, but the overall situation is a bit weird. Let's find your camera and get you on your way, okay? Then I can go through the house and make sure it's secure."

"So, you're going to stay?" she asked doubtfully. "By yourself?"

He gave a faint smile. "I'll be fine."

"Well, the problem with your plan is—" she rose from her crouch and gestured toward the shelves "— I'm not sure where the camera is."

"It's not where you put it?"

"I don't *remember* where I put it." Harmony managed to look embarrassed, defensive, and anxious at the same time. "I really thought it would be here, but it's not."

"But you remembered the exact name of the book

that you put it behind."

Anxiety won. She bit her lip and pushed her hair behind her ears, visibly trying to compose herself. "The book's not here, either. I don't know what I was thinking. The camera is a Canon Rebel. Usually, I treat it like my child. How could I have been so stupid?"

Dale tried not to let his impatience show. "You probably just got a little rattled when you realized someone else was in the house. Are you sure that you brought the camera with you?"

"Of course," Harmony said indignantly.

"You didn't, like, leave it in the car so you could come in and look around first?" Dale was no longer convinced that there even *was* a camera, let alone a car.

"Oh, I get it." Harmony crossed her arms. "You think I'm nutty as a fruitcake, don't you? Or maybe just some weak-nerved female who freaked out because of this dark, scary house?"

When Dale didn't answer, she added, "It's a good thing I have a big, strong misogynist to take care of me, right?"

That seemed a bit harsh.

"Come on," Dale objected. "All I said was—"

"I heard what you said," Harmony retorted. "And what you didn't say. Your insinuation was loud and clear."

Then she huffed and tilted her head. "Of course, we just met, and I'm not exactly disproving your theory by jumping down your throat, am I? What do you do for a living, again? Police officer?"

"Firefighter."

She nodded. "Makes sense. You've got that whole hero-vibe thing. But I think your job has made you jumpy and suspicious."

Again, harsh. "I wouldn't put it exactly like that."

"Well however you might put it, the results are the same. I need to find my camera before I get out of here, and you think I'm nuts and that the camera doesn't even exist. So how do we resolve this, Firefighter Dale?"

Dale rubbed the back of his neck. Harmony had summed up the situation so well that it was hard for him to argue. He wanted to believe her, but he also knew that people he met in strange places were likely to be, well, strange. The very fact that he found her attractive made him even more skeptical. Did he really think she was cute, or was she just setting off alarm bells?

Finally, he decided that only one thing really mattered: "Did you light that fire?"

"No," Harmony answered firmly. "Did you?"

"No," Dale replied, just as firmly.

"I believe you," she said. "And Boo didn't light it, did you boy?"

At the sound of his name, the dog looked up at her and thumped his tail.

"No, you didn't. So, either there *is* another human being in here with us—a human being who, for some reason, chose to frighten us by laying a perfectly lovely fire—or..."

Dale gritted his teeth. He knew what was coming. "Or?"

31

"Or the house is really haunted."

Oh, brother.

"By who?" He gestured to the portrait hanging at the end of the room. "By *him*?"

Harmony's eyes moved to the painting.

"Maybe," she said softly. "He does sort of look like the kind of guy who would come back from the dead and… you know… light cozy fires."

She must have seen something funny in Dale's expression, because she gave a begrudging laugh. "Okay, I admit it sounds ridiculous. But, I mean, look at his face! Don't you think he could be haunting this place?"

Dale hedged. "If I believed in ghosts, he would certainly be a good candidate."

Harmony stared contemplatively at the fire, then gave a little nod like she'd just come to a decision. She said, "I know I'm not crazy. My camera is in here, and I'm going to find it. You don't have to come with me."

Dale didn't like the idea of Harmony roaming the house by herself, especially when he was no longer sure that it was just the two of them.

"I'll come along. Four eyes are better than two." He gestured to Boo. "And six eyes are better than four."

"As long as it's your own choice, and not something that I've guilted you into, then… thanks, I appreciate it." She pointed toward the western side of the building. "I came in through the kitchen."

They searched, but the camera wasn't in the kitchen. Neither was it in the butler's pantry, the dining room, or any of the other rooms on the first floor. On the plus side, Dale saw absolutely no sign that there was someone else in the house, and that whole "I sense a presence" feeling was gone. He supposed that if Harmony could misplace an expensive camera, she could light a fire and forget about it. Maybe he should chalk it up to her artistic personality.

But Harmony, herself, was not particularly reassured. "I just can't believe this. It's beyond ridiculous." She frowned. "Maybe I *am* nutty as a fruitcake."

Boo, who had shadowed them through the house, whined faintly at the frustration in Harmony's voice. The three of them were in the foyer, standing outside the parlor where light from the fireplace glowed dully. Dale knew he should check it, make sure that he didn't accidentally burn the house down. But his attention was drawn to the curving staircase, and to the banister up above. He almost expected to see someone in the gallery up there, looking down on them.

Before he could stop himself, he said, "We haven't checked upstairs yet."

"No, we haven't," Harmony replied. "But at this point I think I should just come back tomorrow when it's daylight. It seems really dangerous to be poking around here at night."

"You're probably right," he answered slowly. "I'm sorry we couldn't find the Canon."

"Me too," she sighed. "But I guess it's time to admit defeat, at least for tonight. Thanks for your help."

She held out her hand in a farewell shake, but Dale hesitated. This was what he wanted, right? She was going, and he could be alone, without having to worry about her.

And yet, he heard himself saying, "Are you sure you don't want to take a quick look upstairs? I have this weird feeling."

"Weird" was definitely the word for it.

Harmony dropped her hand and looked uncertainly at the darkness at the top of the stairs. "Go upstairs in a haunted house after dark?" she mused. "Usually, I'd jump at an idea that ridiculous."

Dale pursed his lips. "Maybe it's not the smartest move. I just thought it might be worthwhile to check, you know? I mean, you were up there, tonight, weren't you?"

"Yes, I was. And I guess it's a good idea to be thorough." She raised a finger. "But if we meet any ghosts, remember this was your idea."

Harmony turned and headed across the foyer, with Boo trailing behind. After a moment, Dale followed too.

Harmony was carrying Dale's electric lantern. As she started up the stairs, it shone an eerie light on the paintings that hung along the staircase.

"Are these people all Wicklow family members?" Dale asked.

"I think so," Harmony said.

She stopped halfway up the stairs and peered at one of the paintings. "Isn't it strange how faces can look so familiar? I swear this man looks just like the guy in that old Carpet Warehouse commercial."

Dale glanced at the painting, but all he saw was a harmless face, pale and a tad pudgy. He shrugged. "I couldn't say."

As he shifted, the step creaked slightly under his feet. But despite a few squeaks and squawks, the staircase seemed solid, just like the rest of the house. "If I had the money," he mused, "I'd buy this place and fix it up."

"I think everyone who comes here feels that way," Harmony said. She trailed a finger lightly on the wall. "The house gets under your skin."

He ascended the next stair to show her that they could keep going, but Harmony didn't budge. Instead, she turned to face him.

She asked, "So, how come you have nothing better to do than spend Halloween in an abandoned old house?"

He laughed, surprised. "You really have a way with words, don't you?"

She looked embarrassed but stuck out her chin defensively. "I didn't mean to be rude. And I know you said that the mayor asked for your help. But I still think this is kind of a silly way to spend your evening."

"Well, gee, thanks for not being rude," Dale said. "And I guess I shouldn't point out that you're *also* spending your evening this way."

"I came here for my art."

"Yeah, okay. And you care so much about your art that you lost your camera? Please."

He was teasing, but her chin trembled at his words, and suddenly all her cheekiness drained away. "I still can't believe I could do that." She put her hands to her face. "If that camera is really lost…"

"Hey." He touched her arm. "Don't worry, we'll find it. I mean, it's got to be here somewhere, right?"

Harmony lowered her hands, and Dale was abruptly aware that they were standing very close together. He was a step below her, which put them just on eye level. And on lip level.

Harmony's eyes floated down to his mouth, and Dale swallowed. She had a tiny scar on her chin, a little crescent of white. He had the urge to touch it. His hand released her arm and started to drift upward.

Harmony backed away, stumbling slightly as she moved up three steps, just out of reach. Dale, confused, took a step downward. There was now a respectable distance between them. Boo remained where he was, looking from one unfathomable human to the other, and back again.

"We should go ahead and look upstairs," Harmony said hurriedly. "It's getting late, and…"

"Yeah," Dale said. "Absolutely."

She moved away, and he took a deep breath. What was wrong with him? Harmony had a boyfriend; that made her officially off-limits. And even if she hadn't been attached, Dale wasn't in the habit of hitting on women an hour after he'd met them.

He looked down at the dog, who had waited for him while Harmony resumed her climb up the staircase. Boo wagged his tail and blinked his shining eyes.

"I know," Dale muttered. "I need to get myself together."

Dale

The dog and man went together up the stairs. Harmony was waiting at the top.

Dale said immediately, "I'm sorry about that… whatever it was."

"Oh, no worries." Her reply was a little too quick. "This is kind of a peculiar situation, right? And peculiar responses are normal in peculiar situations."

He huffed an uncertain laugh. "I guess so."

Harmony cleared her throat. "When I was up here earlier, the only place I remember going was the master bedroom. It's got a semi-famous mantelpiece, and I wanted to take pictures of it. That's my last clear memory of my camera, which makes it the logical place to start looking, right?"

"Logical place," Dale agreed. "Lead the way."

She gave him a final, undefined glance, then strode

off down the hallway. He followed, and Boo moved with them.

Hoping to restore a bit of normalcy, Dale asked, "Why is the mantelpiece semi-famous?"

"It has a face carved in it. Supposedly if you ask it questions, you'll get an answer."

Okay, so much for normal.

Harmony said, "You really don't know much about this place, do you?"

"I got the lowdown from the town's historical society today," Dale answered, feeling defensive. "I know that the Wicklows made their money from forging iron ore. After the Civil War, the mine went bust, and so did the family. But the quote-unquote 'hauntings'? No, I didn't pay attention."

"You don't believe in ghosts?"

"I've seen a lot of death," Dale replied, more grimly than he'd intended. "I've never seen any sign of something beyond it."

That effectively ended the conversation, and they traversed the remainder of the corridor in silence.

The master bedroom was large and ornate. There was a four-poster bed which looked like it might have held a canopy at one time. An old mattress still lay on its frame. Doors to the closet and bathroom stood partially open, revealing slices of darkness that weren't penetrated by either Dale's flashlight beam or the light from Harmony's lantern.

Across from the bed was the semi-famous fireplace. When his flashlight found it, Dale could see why the carving might seize the imagination of ghost-hunting types. It was the face of a young woman: eyes half-closed as if in blissful meditation, lips parted as if she might speak at any moment. The mantel was supported on either side by carvings of cherubs. It brought a fragment of poetry to Dale's mind, but he couldn't quite place the line.

Beside him, Harmony murmured, "'May flights of angels sing thee to thy rest.'"

He looked at her.

"It's from *Hamlet*," she said.

"That's fitting." Dale tried to keep the irony from his voice. "He saw a ghost, didn't he?"

"Lots of people do," Harmony replied, unruffled. She smiled placidly. "Do you want to ask her a question?"

"Sure." Dale crossed the wide hardwood floor and stood in front of the fireplace. He leaned over, hands on knees, and spoke cheerily. "Hey there, inanimate piece of wood. Here's my question: Where's Harmony's camera?"

Harmony had come up alongside him. He could almost hear her roll her eyes. But he didn't hear an answer, ghostly or otherwise, to his query.

Dale straightened. "Well, I guess that theory has been tested and disproven," he said. "Should we try the old-fashioned way and just look for it?"

"You don't have to be a jerk about it," Harmony grumbled.

"Sorry."

Dale rolled his neck, heard a crack. The situation was officially wearing on his nerves. The weird fire and the hypnotic tile floor and the stray dog and the strange but fascinating woman standing next to him. He just wanted to rewind his life to dinner on the previous night, and choose a different course. If he'd just accepted the arrangement that Jenner had proposed, then he, Dale, would be in a brightly lit firehouse at that moment, instead of in this crazy house.

He heard a growl, and looked around for Boo, wondering if maybe the dog had cornered a rat. But Boo was still in the hallway. His head was low, and the hackles on his back were raised. The dog bared his teeth and growled again.

Great, Dale thought. *What now?*

"Dale," Harmony whispered.

He looked her way. Her face had gone quite pale, and her eyes were wide and round. Her hair even looked redder than before, but that may have been because of the difference in the light.

The difference in the light.

Dale turned slowly. Across the room, the closet door stood ajar. He was sure it had been closed when they entered. But it was wide open now. And light was emanating from deep inside it.

"There's no electricity here," he said without thinking, "and the bulbs wouldn't last that long, anyway."

As if that mattered. The gleam inside the closet wasn't electrical. And it wasn't a fire, either. It was just… a glow.

Harmony took a few steps forward.

"Where are you going?" Dale hissed.

She looked back at him, eyes confused, but then

turned and started advancing again.

From nowhere came the smell of lemons. And suddenly, Dale knew what was going on. He laughed. He actually laughed, because he had been too dumb to guess it until right then.

It *was* all a joke, after all. It was some kind of strange aversion therapy, or maybe just a Halloween gag. But everything that had happened was some kind of setup. And Jenner was probably waiting inside the closet, with a big grin on his face.

"Oh my God." Dale followed Harmony, still laughing. He called, "Jenner, where are you? And did you really think this would help me get past my late-October blues?"

He reached the closet door and looked inside. The space was empty, illuminated by an unidentifiable source. For a moment, he wondered if Harmony had disappeared, like the woman in the town hall. But then his eyes found another, smaller door on the opposite wall. Light streamed from the other side. That must be where Harmony had gone.

"Okay, guys, that's enough." Dale crossed the closet in four steps and moved through the other door. "Honestly, I'm flattered you would go to all this trouble just for me, but really you..."

He halted in his tracks. "...shouldn't have."

As Dale finished the sentence, he knew how wrong he had been.

This wasn't a joke. It wasn't a prank. It wasn't a setup. He didn't know what it was.

This was something he could not explain.

The room beyond the closet was also small, befitting its entrance. At one time, it might have been a storage room. Dale could easily imagine it full of hat boxes and cedar trunks. But at the moment, it was empty except for a narrow bed covered with a white sheet. And on the sheet, stretched out full, with eyes closed, was Harmony. She and the bed were surrounded by an unearthly light. The camera lay forgotten at her feet.

He heard a moan, small and stricken, barely enough to flicker a candle. He turned to his right and saw a second Harmony, standing in the corner.

He quickly looked back at the bed and saw Harmony, again. Her hair, the shade of autumn leaves, streamed around her pale face. The scar on her chin stood out brightly in the strange light.

Dale once more turned his head to the right and saw Harmony, standing in the corner. She wore an expression of utter horror, and of sudden, dreadful understanding.

Harmony was looking at her own body, lying there on that bed.

She turned terrified eyes up to his face.

"I guess I'm the ghost," she croaked weakly. "Boo."

CHAPTER
SIX

Harmony

Poor Dale. Poor handsome, heroic Dale, stout of heart and square of jaw. He was trapped in a house with a walking, talking spirit.

I mean, that's what I was, right? He knew it, and I guess I did too. I was the ghost. I was the thing that haunted Wicklow House.

"Boo," I had said to him, in what I still think is an ultra-cool response to the whole crazy scenario.

For a moment, I was calm. I was a placid blue ocean under a serene blue sky.

Then the moment passed, and I freaked out.

"What the *actual* hell is going on?" I shrieked, and I immediately wished I hadn't. When my voice hit its highest pitch, the wind kicked up and howled in the bedroom chimney, and the panes rattled in the windows.

I cringed, but I couldn't shut up. "Am I a *ghost*, Dale? Am I *dead*?"

Dale waited for the fresh burst of wind to die down.

"Of course not," he said, with such an air of common sense that I immediately felt better. "You must have a twin sister, or something like that."

"A twin sister that I don't know anything about?"

"It's happened before."

Aaaand I felt worse again. He clearly thought I was bonkers. Or lying. Or both.

He picked up my body's hand, put professional fingers to the spot where the pulse would be. He set the hand carefully down and touched the side of the—my—neck.

"Well?" I asked desperately.

"No pulse," he said. "But the body's still warm."

He looked shaken, and who could blame him? Best-case scenario, he'd been talking to a dead lady for the past hour. Worst-case scenario? He was in the house with a twin-killing madwoman.

I opened my mouth to say something calm, sane, and reassuring. What came out was, "This is another fine mess you've gotten us into."

He laughed, and I breathed a little easier.

Wait, *was* I breathing? My chest was moving, so maybe I was. But why would I need to breathe? It's not like I had actual human lungs, or blood to oxygenate, or veins to carry oxygen to cells. Or cells, for that matter.

But I must have been breathing, because I started to hyperventilate. I tried to gulp air, but it didn't go anywhere, because I had nowhere for it to go. I leaned over, hands on knees. I was trying to breathe and unable to breathe and I was wheezing and shaking and it was terrible. I felt like I was going to die, and yet apparently, I was already dead.

"Calm down," Dale ordered. He came over and stood next to me, but didn't try to touch me—could he touch me? "Stop thinking about trying to breathe. Come on, let's get you out of this closet."

He tried to lead me away—and yes, he was touching me, because he was guiding me out by my shoulders; how did this being a ghost thing work, anyway?—and I freaked in a new way.

"My body!" I cried. "I can't leave it."

"It's not going anywhere," Dale said sternly. He gripped my shoulders tighter and walked me out into the big bedroom.

Out there, with the high ceilings and the tall windows, I felt my chest expand, and my panic began to ebb.

"Okay," I said, trying to wrap my mind around the situation. "Okay. I guess—I guess I'm a ghost."

"I don't believe that." But he didn't look convinced.

I wanted to sigh, but I was afraid it would set off another bout of phantom hyperventilation. I wanted to sit somewhere, but I was afraid I'd fall through the chair. So, I tried leaning against one of the balusters of the bed. And yes, it held me. I felt the cool surface and the grain of the wood against my cheek.

Dale stood in the center of the room, hands held up as if he were preparing to conduct an orchestra. I could almost see the questions tumbling around in his head. They would be the same ones tumbling around in mine. He dropped his hands and spoke.

"Okay," he said, making me wish we could both find a different word to use. "Let's look at this whole thing logically. Okay?"

"Fine," I answered, breaking the pattern. "Let's logically look at how I am somehow dead in the closet and alive out here."

He regarded me with composed caring, and I thought about what a good emergency responder he must be. In a time of crisis (any crisis, not just the one where I was dead and yet alive) his face would be the one I would want to see.

"Let's take the obvious question first," Dale said. "Is it possible that you do have a sister you've never met? Or do you have any female relatives who look like you?"

I shook my head slowly. "I have two brothers. No sister. And all my female cousins are a lot older than I am."

"How much do you remember about what happened to you?"

"Nothing," I said miserably. "Only what I told you earlier tonight. I parked out back, I came in through the kitchen, walked around taking pictures, and then I heard you poking around."

"That's it?" he asked.

"That's it," I affirmed.

But then it wasn't. There was a flash of something. A face? No, a name.

"Orrin," I said. "Orrin was here."

"Okay." Dale reverted to pattern. "Okay. That's good. Orrin who?"

Again, I shook my head.

"Was he a friend of yours? Did he come with you? Was he already in the house?"

"I don't *know*," I cried. The windowpanes rattled.

Dale sighed and came over to the bed. He sank down on the mattress and looked at me. "I'm sorry," he said. "I don't know what to do, here."

I must admit, I was feeling a little sorry for myself. Tears gathered behind my eyes, and I wondered what they were made of. Phantom salt water?

"How did I die, Dale? And why didn't anyone come looking for me?"

"Who says they didn't?" His face was serious. He sat slowly down onto the old mattress. The springs squealed but held him. He pulled a phone out of his pocket. "I think it's time we asked the internet about you."

He swiped and tapped, and then sat and read. I waited patiently. It's not like I was getting any older.

At last, he looked up, and gestured for me to sit next to him. I did, carefully. I didn't fall through the bed, but the springs didn't squeak, either. I was there, but not there. It was an odd feeling.

"They did look for you," he said softly. "They even looked here."

He tilted his phone so I could see it. My face shone up from the screen. It was a picture that my mother had taken on my first day of college. I frowned. I hated that picture.

Dale quoted the text: "'Harmony Lowell, last seen at State College on Halloween night…'"

"Six years ago," I whispered. "Six years?"

I looked up at him, and he nodded.

"Apparently, yes. I'm so sorry, Harmony," he said. "Do you want to read this?"

The details didn't matter now. "My parents," I moaned. "My poor mom. She doesn't know that I'm—I'm—whatever I am."

"According to this article, you told your boyfriend you were going to Wicklow House to take pictures. People came here and looked for you," he said. "You don't remember that?"

"No. I thought I'd only been here for a few hours, not…" I trailed off again. Seventy-two months. Hundreds of days. I had been dead all that time. Why couldn't I remember what had happened?

My hand reached automatically for Boo, hoping to feel the reassuring softness of his fur beneath my hand. But he wasn't there. I looked toward the hallway, where I'd last seen him. It was empty. He must have run off. Guess I couldn't blame him for that.

Dale was still talking. "They didn't find you, and they didn't find your car," he said. I tried to focus on the words that were coming out of his mouth, but it was difficult. My eyes wandered around the room, taking in the rich wallpaper which was mildewed and hanging in shreds in places. Water stains on the walls. Dust everywhere. How could I have spent the last six years here?

"Is it possible that someone killed me?" I asked suddenly. "Killed me, hid my body, moved my car? I mean, that has to be what happened, right? And that's why I'm haunting this house, because I want my death to be avenged?"

"Are you asking me or telling me?"

I thought about it. "Yes to both. And no to both."

He sighed, and I envied him the gust of wind that came out through his lips. Flesh people had no idea how lucky they were.

"Obviously, I have no idea why you're here or what happened to you," he said. "I don't even believe in ghosts, which is why I agreed to spend the night in this place. And yet, here you are, all separated from your body, walking and talking and giving me attitude."

"This isn't your problem, is that what you're telling me?"

"No, I'm not saying that. But does it even matter how you got here? Shouldn't we be talking about what's really important?"

"And that is?"

"How are we going to get you *out* of here?"

Before I could reply, his eyes widened, and he stared at me in a way that would have really frightened me if I hadn't just found out I was dead.

"What's wrong?" I asked.

"Look at your hand," he whispered.

I did, then I moaned. The wind flared up around the house again. I held my hand up to the light, and I could see the outline of the door on the other side.

"I'm fading away."

49

Desperate, I looked at him. "I'm disappearing," I cried. "Help me. What do we do?"

His response was immediate. "We go. We leave the house."

"What about my body?"

"We'll take it with us. Come on." He moved as if to take my hand, but then apparently thought better of it. Instead, he stood up.

"Why should we leave?" I asked.

"Think about it. A search party came to this house and didn't find your body or the car. The police were here more than once, and there have even been ghost hunting parties coming through here since you disappeared. None of them saw any sign of you. But tonight, Halloween, you're here, and I can see you."

"You think it's some kind of All Hallow's magic?"

"I don't know what to think, and part of me doesn't believe any of this. But it's possible that this might be the only night you're visible. It might be our only chance to get you out."

I hesitated, and he snapped, "We don't have a lot of time to argue, here. Now come on."

He marched across the room, through the closet into the chamber behind, and scooped up my body. It made me feel dizzy to watch, but he did it without hesitation. The body still glowed, casting him in a golden light as he moved.

"Come on," he said. "We'll run now, ask questions later."

He didn't give me a chance to argue. He carried my body out of the room, along the hall and down the stairs. I tripped after him, calling for Boo, wanting the reassurance that only a friendly animal can provide.

As I moved, I became aware that I couldn't feel the floor under my feet. I didn't want to think about that, didn't want to wonder if I even still *had* feet.

Dale reached the first floor when I was halfway down the stairs. He looked over his shoulder to make sure that I was behind him, opened the door, and started to cross the threshold.

I paused, suddenly sure that he wouldn't make it to the outside.

And he didn't. He hefted my body, moved forward with determination, and bounced back like he'd been tossed into a giant cube of Jell-O. My head lolled in his arms, giving me phantom queasiness as I watched.

Dale stepped away, regarded the rectangle of night that loomed beyond the doorway, and resolutely sallied forward again. He rebounded backward a second time, repelled by some invisible barrier.

"Shulman," I said abruptly.

I was still on the stairs. Dale turned and gaped up at me. "What?"

"Orrin's last name. It was Shulman."

"Oh, great," Dale said, straight-faced. "That's helpful, thanks."

Given the situation, I couldn't help but feel that his sarcasm was a little bit overdone. But before I could tell him so, he had gathered my body more closely in his arms, then turned his rear end to the door and tried backing over the threshold. When he hit the line between indoors and outdoors, I heard a voice.

51

"Stuck," Orrin had said.

At the same time, Dale cursed. He had bounced off the doorway again. He gazed longingly out the open door. Cool autumn air drifted in, carrying that wistful damp-leaf smell. Dale's car was visible on the driveway, barely a dozen paces away. Freedom was tantalizingly close, and yet completely unreachable.

Defeat was starting to creep into his stance, as he strained under the weight of my corpse (now *there's* a sentence you don't get to say every day!). Suddenly a light came on in his eyes.

"The kitchen window," he said. "We'll go out the way you came in. Maybe that will work."

But it wouldn't, and all at once I knew why.

"No," I told him. "I can't leave, and neither can my body."

"Don't give up," he said, seemingly desperate. "We'll just try it and—"

"Dale, I'm so sorry," I said sadly. "It won't work."

"How do you know?"

"Because I do." I looked at my hands. They were solid once more: a perfect simulation of flesh. I nodded toward my body. "Put that thing down and come here. I'll explain everything."

Dale gazed up at me, frustration written on his features. Then he glanced down at my face, cradled in the crook of his arm. His shoulders sagged in resignation. He carried my body to a long bench in the foyer and laid it down. One of my hands flopped onto the intricate tile floor. He picked it up gently, almost reverently, and placed it on my stomach.

"This can't be real," I heard him mutter. "There's no evidence of death. The body is warm and pliant, there's been no decay."

"That's because it isn't completely dead," I said loudly. "Come on up here. I have something to show you."

"This is ridiculous." He stalked up the stairs, mouth tight and eyes blazing, and held out a hand to me. "Save your story for later. Let's get out of here."

My phantom heart was a lead weight in my phantom chest. "I wish we could. I really do. But we can't."

Slowly, slowly I reached out and touched his hand. "And it's not my story. It's yours."

CHAPTER
SEVEN

Dale

Dale didn't believe any of this. He couldn't. This situation with the house and Harmony was like being marooned on a buoy in the middle of the ocean. The water of lunacy crashed around him, spraying him with cold, salty water. But he refused to fall in.

Mentally, he wiped the mist from his face. He had to get Harmony *and* the body out of the house. Outside, in the real world, he would be back on solid ground, and things would return to normal. They had to. And if Harmony wouldn't come out of danger willingly, if she felt compelled to swim in the madness, then he would drag her out of harm's way.

And so, when she slipped her cold fingers into his hand, he grasped tightly and tried to pull her toward him. But instead, he found himself being pulled up four steps to where she stood. His feet moved, his body ascended: he didn't have any choice in the matter.

As they once again stood eye to eye, he saw that Harmony's features were composed, almost calm, and she appeared to be fully corporeal again. She gestured to a painting on the wall.

"Remember this guy?" she asked.

Dale wanted to give her a piece of his mind, but he found himself turning and looking at the painting. It was the one they had looked at on their way upstairs. "The guy who looks like he was in a carpet commercial?"

"That's Orrin," she told him. "Orrin Shulman. He was here when I arrived six years ago."

"So, he's haunting this place too?" Dale couldn't believe he had just said that. The crazy-water was starting to seep through his clothes. He fought to stay dry, to stay sane.

Harmony laid a finger on the frame of the painting. Dust shifted, supporting Dale's perception that she was a physical presence in the room.

"Not anymore." She answered his question quietly.

"Harmony, would you please just tell me what's going on?"

"I don't know. I mean, I remember all of it." Her eyes were hazy as she struggled to recollect. "I have a clear memory of coming to the house. That part still feels like it was just earlier this evening. I parked out back and climbed in through the kitchen window, like I told you. The light was perfect. I took a lot of pictures. And then, at some point, Orrin was there."

Dale tried to go with the flow. "You mean he materialized, or something?"

"No, it was more like the way that you and I met. He was in the house, and we started talking. I don't know how I first realized he was a ghost, whether he told me, or I just figured it out. The only thing I know for sure is that he was trapped here, just like I am now."

"So, what happened?" Dale made a rolling motion with his hand, needing her to get on with it and drop the other shoe.

"He told me he was stuck, and there was only one way for him to escape." She swallowed visibly. "Someone had to take his place."

And there it was. "You mean…"

"I mean the only way for Orrin to be free was for someone else to become trapped."

From the top of the stairs came a sharp, urgent bark. Dale and Harmony turned their gaze in that direction. Boo stood poised on the top step, eyes wide and bright, staring at them. He frisked in place, a movement that was less playful than it was entreating.

Dale started toward the dog, automatically responding to the appeal, but Harmony stopped him.

"Wait." She put a hand on his arm. "Look at this."

She pointed to the next painting on the wall, one step up from Orrin's. Dale saw, to his horror, that it was Harmony's face framed in the painting.

As things finally fell into place, his eyes moved even farther up the stairs, and he saw his own features—lightly sketched, but still distinctly his—in the next frame.

Boo whined, a thin and worried sound that deepened into a low moan.

"The sun has set," Harmony said gravely. "And you're caught here, just like me, until sunrise."

Dale didn't so much hear her words as feel them in the marrow of his bones. A deep, resonant chill vibrated through him. He heard himself ask a question. "What happens at sunrise?"

She paused, then said, "You can go. But I'll have to stay here."

The waters of madness finally reached his skin, saturating his pores and making his head swim. He was drenched in the insanity, and could hold out against it no longer. He loosed his grip on the buoy, and let himself sink.

CHAPTER
EIGHT

Harmony

Dale's face paled. His eyes went blank and distant. I could see that he was spinning with the craziness of the situation.

"Stay with me." I wanted to make it a command, but it came out sounding more like a plea.

On the landing above us, Boo barked again, like he was seconding my words. I patted my leg, hoping he would come down and offer some comfort. He descended a few steps, paused, then ran right back up again.

Dale shook his head sharply, as if to clear it. He reached out and grasped the railing, like a blind man trying to get his bearings.

A moment later, he spoke. "I'm having a very hard time believing any of this."

"You don't have to believe something for it to be

true," I said.

My words elicited a weak smile, then a half-laugh.

"That's deep," he said.

"Thanks."

He closed his eyes and drew in a deep breath, visibly summoning strength. When he opened them again, I was relieved to see Firefighter Dale, grim and determined, looking back at me. He got right down to business.

He nodded to the image that I had shown him. "So, that's Orrin." Then his fingers reached out and lightly touched the frame of my own picture. "And this is you."

"Right."

He gestured at the downward side of the staircase. "And all of these people are the ones who have come before?"

"I believe so, yes."

"So, who was the first?"

I blinked. Why hadn't I thought to ask that, myself?

"Let's go and see," I said.

Back down the steps we went, passing images of men and women, every age and color of the rainbow. It was difficult to fathom that they had all been in my shoes, stuck here and just wanting to go home. What had happened to them? Had they all made it out?

I didn't want to think about it. I only knew that, before sunrise came, I was going to find a way for Dale to leave. I might be trapped here, but there was no way I'd let him suffer the same fate. And hopefully, he would take Boo with him. The two of them seemed to need each other in some way that I didn't fully understand.

I was thinking about this when I realized that Dale had already reached the first floor. I hurried down to join him.

"Guess who," Dale said grimly.

I looked at the face that occupied the first frame on this sad parade of souls. I wasn't at all surprised to see J. W. Wicklow glaring back at me.

"Of course," I said. "This *is* his house. Who else would be the first to haunt it?"

"I guess it does make sense." Dale crossed his arms. "Now, what's our next step?"

"You're asking me?"

"You're the only ghost here. I mean, as far as I know."

I was flummoxed. "Yeah, but it's not like I have any idea what's going on. I didn't even know I was a ghost until ten minutes ago."

"Well, nothing in my emergency responder training prepared me for this situation, Harmony," he huffed. "A little help would be nice."

"We're both figuring this out as we go along, *Dale*," I flared. I was mimicking his tone, but my irritation was real. "I'm telling you everything I know."

He studied me. "Are you?"

Wow.

"What are you implying?" I tried to sound angry, but in truth I was hurt.

His eyes remained on my face, pensive and uncertain, for a moment longer. Then he blew out a breath and looked away.

"I don't know," he replied. "Nothing. Everything."

"Do you really think I would lie to you in a crazy situation like this?"

"My head says it's possible. My heart says no."

I tried to ignore the way my pulse skipped when he used the word "heart." Stupid romantic impulses, always intruding at the wrong time. What did I think was going to happen, we were going to fall in love and live happily, *hauntedly,* ever after? I needed to worry about living at all, and then maybe I could start to think about what came next.

My eyes drifted upward, looking for Boo, but he was gone again.

"And what does your gut tell you?" I asked Dale.

"That I'm hungry."

His answer was so unexpected that I laughed, and after a second, he joined in.

"I can't help it," he said. "It's late, and I haven't had dinner."

"Fair enough." He was only human, after all. "Let's have a snack break, *then* figure out how to fight the evil lurking inside the old dark house."

"It's what Scooby and Shaggy would do," he dead-panned. "Speaking of which…"

Dale whistled for Boo, but I told him the dog had run off. I kept my voice light, knowing that Boo was probably safer in this old place than Dale or I would ever be. But I didn't like the fact that he kept running away somewhere.

Neither, apparently, did Dale, who replied gravely. "You need to train your pet. It's not safe to let him roam like that."

I followed Dale into the living room, where his cooler still sat with his backpack and sleeping bag.

"He'll be fine," I said, hoping it was true. "That dog is smarter than both of us put together. And he's not my pet, he's yours. He found you first, remember?"

"I wish his real owners would come and get him," Dale said. "Whether it's those teenagers that the mayor was worried about, or just some family nearby who have a weird sense of humor about pet names."

He stirred up the fire and added another log. The resulting flames, along with the electric lantern that I set on the floor, did a good job of illuminating the room.

Dale switched off his flashlight, settled on his sleeping bag and opened the cooler. I peeled back a corner of dust cover on the old sofa and perched on the edge. I couldn't help but wonder about the physics of my spectral state. My body was in the foyer, on the bench. Yet here I was, interacting with the physical universe as if I was still walking around in that bag of bones. It messed with the head.

Dale had pulled a ham sandwich and bottle of Coke from the cooler. He held them out to me, but I shook my head.

"Not hungry?" he asked.

"Non-corporeal," I reminded him. "No need for food."

"Oh, right." He unwrapped the sandwich and took a bite. As he chewed, he asked, "So, what's *your* gut telling *you* about this situation?"

That was a good question. I replied slowly, trying to feel my way through. "I don't know. I don't think I was ever very good at listening to my gut. Believe it or not, I was kind of a by-the-numbers type when I was alive. I started off studying accounting a few years ago, but switched to photography."

It occurred to me that my accounting studies were actually more than "a few" years ago, but I skipped it. I didn't feel like getting into an existential discussion about the passage of time for the nearly departed.

"Why did you switch?" Dale asked.

"My boyfriend proposed."

The reply came automatically, out of some recess of memory not previously accessed.

I sat up straight. "Wow. I just remembered that. My boyfriend proposed, and I kind of panicked, thinking about being a married accountant. It doesn't get more 'settled' than that, does it? I wasn't ready to feel settled. So I told him I had to think about it for a little while. Then I switched my major to photography. And that's why I came here to take pictures."

"Which turned out to be a great decision," Dale said helpfully. "Because otherwise you never would have met me."

It was a good thing to say. I'd just started to feel sorry for myself. But his words made me laugh. "Best decision I ever made," I agreed.

He crumpled up the empty sandwich wrapper and tucked it into the cooler. He placed the Coke lid on the bottle, then moved to sit next to me on the sofa.

"I know this is a supremely weird situation," he said.

"But we *will* get out of it."

His words were intended to make me feel better, but his very kindness made my eyes fill with tears. I blinked them away.

"Of course we will," I said stoutly. "I've never doubted it for a second."

Unfortunately, my lion-hearted sentiment was punctuated by an extremely chicken-hearted wobble in my voice.

Dale laced the fingers of his right hand through the fingers of my left.

"I almost believed you," he said.

A dimple danced in his cheek as he tried not to smile, and my pulse did that skipping thing again.

With his free hand, he smoothed the hair away from my forehead. His gaze moved from my hair to my eyes, and settled on my lips. The fire in the hearth was dying, yet the air between Dale and I grew warm, and seemed to contract, pulling us toward one another. Our mouths grew closer until we were millimeters from kissing.

And that was when Boo bounced onto the scene, licking us both smack in our pieholes.

CHAPTER
NINE

Dale

Dale leapt to his feet. The dog's sudden reappearance was like a bucket of ice dumped over his head. Had he really been about to kiss Harmony? Kiss a girl that he'd just met in a weird old house? Kiss a *ghost*?

He didn't know if that was creepy or cool.

Harmony laughed, seemingly unaffected. When he turned back her way, Boo was half up on her lap. His canine elbows rested on her legs, while his back paws were still on the floor, and she was rubbing him behind the ears. With the flickering firelight, it was a warm, homey scene that made Dale long for the kind of cozy home life he had never known.

"I've never been smooch-blocked by a dog before," Harmony said. "Guess there really is a first time for everything."

Her gaze zeroed in on Dale's expression. "Oh, hey, are you freaked out by what almost happened?"

"A bit, yeah." He was probably risking offending her with his honesty, but he couldn't summon the strength of mind to lie. "Not the best time or place, you know?"

A look of hurt crossed her features, but she nodded with understanding. "Stupid romantic impulses, always intruding at the wrong moment."

He was about to speak, hoping to say something which might make things seem a bit more normal between them, although the very idea of normal seemed incomprehensible, when Boo licked her again.

Harmony chuckled. "Speaking of intruding at the wrong moment."

She nudged him away and stood up, brushing the dog fur off her phantom lap. When she looked at Dale, her eyes were clear.

"Okay," she said. "You've had your snack. Let's get back to business."

Suddenly, Dale was so tired that he could barely stand, and his vision was almost hazy. He picked up the bottle of Coke and chugged it, hoping for a rush. He could barely keep up with the events of this strange night, but he was glad that he wasn't going through it alone.

He put the empty bottle back in his cooler and straightened. Back to business, as Harmony had said.

"So," he began.

"So," Harmony echoed encouragingly.

He wasn't sure how to continue, so he cleared his throat and thought out loud. "J.W. Wicklow?"

"Right," Harmony confirmed.

"What's up with that guy?"

"Good question," she laughed. "Maybe Boo knows."

She looked down for the dog, but he had slipped away.

"Oh, for Pete's sake, not again," Harmony sighed. "You really need to put a leash on your dog."

"He's not my dog," Dale said automatically. And yet, it was with an owner's voice that he called out, "Boo? Boo!"

From the foyer came a responding yip. Harmony lifted the lantern, and they turned to see Boo, halfway up the stairs, with his head poking through the banister. When he saw that he had their attention, he yipped again, then gave a commanding bark.

"Maybe he found a clue." Harmony sounded amused.

"Tonight, I'd say anything is possible."

Dale switched on his flashlight and fished around in his backpack until he found a bundle of cord. It was orange nylon, very strong yet soft to the touch. He used his pocketknife to cut a length of it, then started across the foyer.

"Fine. I'll put a leash on him," he muttered. Before Harmony could speak, he called over his shoulder, "And, no, he's still not my dog."

Dale went up the first half of the staircase where Boo was waiting with a wagging tail and lolling grin. Holding the flashlight under his arm, he looped the nylon through the ring on Boo's collar, tying it into a gnat hitch to keep it fastened. He looped the other end into a handle and secured it with a figure eight knot.

"You're not going anywhere, poochie." He roughed the dog's ears and chucked him under the chin.

From the bottom of the stairs, Harmony said, "If this was a movie, we'd go to the local historian and find out all of Wicklow's sins and secrets."

She was standing at the bottom of the stairs, gazing at Wicklow's image. Beyond her, night loomed inky through the uncovered foyer windows. Haze still seemed to hover at the edges of Dale's vision.

He shook his head and tried to focus. "Then we'd have to find the source of his trauma and resolve it."

"Or find his bones and burn them. Oh, wait." Harmony pinched her lip. "What about his portrait in the library? The one of him in the graveyard? It makes more sense now, I guess."

"Yeah, for sure," Dale said absently.

Was the haze in his vision getting thicker? Great, just great. Because the one thing missing from this experience was some kind of neurological episode.

He pushed on with the discussion. "Any chance there's a clue in there?"

"Couldn't hurt to look."

Harmony started to turn in the direction of the library. But she had barely rotated a few degrees when the haze began to condense and gather in the corners of the room. Slowly, slowly, it drifted across the floor.

Harmony stopped short, then backed up, retreating a few stairs upward. "Dale," she whispered.

"I see it," Dale said.

His relief at the fact that he wasn't hallucinating

68

was quickly vanquished by the utter supernatural terror that assaulted him. Tonight, he'd met a ghost. He'd seen a body that was dead and yet not dead. Now, there in front of him, an unknown phenomenon was creeping in his direction.

He felt frozen, his skin icy and puckered with goosebumps. His heart raced and blood pounded in his ears. He wanted to do nothing more than run and hide. But he descended three steps until he stood in front of Harmony, between her and the whatever-it-was.

The haze reached the bottom step, swirling like misty creek water. Something tugged on his hand, and for a moment he thought it was Harmony. But it was Boo, on the other end of the leash, straining to get upstairs. The dog was smarter than he was.

In the foyer, the mist seemed to solidify in some places, and Dale realized that it was piling up: rising from the floor, gathering as it went, until it began to form pillars at the base of the stairs.

Boo whimpered. Dale and Harmony backed up, ascending slowly in a clumsy choreography.

As they moved, the pillar closest to them changed shape, began to form into something that looked almost human. Dale could make out shoulders, and a head. The smell of lemons filled the air.

"Dale," Harmony said again, more urgently this time.

"I know."

As he watched, transfixed, the pillar began to form features. Phantom eyes turned in his direction. Boo yanked again, yipping and crying in desperation.

"*Dale*," Harmony cried, tugging on his shirt.

"Go," he said. The eyes fixed on his and began to burn with blue flame. "Harmony, go."

She went, and he was right behind her, with Boo leading the way. Up the stairs, and down a hallway, moving on instinct. When they had turned several corners and were out of sight of the glow from the foyer, they stopped to catch their breath.

"What was that?" Harmony gasped. "Was it a ghost?"

She seemed to realize the irony in her question because she huffed out a quick laugh. "And if it was, why would I be scared of it?"

Dale didn't answer. His mind had temporarily gone numb. That figure, those eyes… he knew those eyes from somewhere.

"Are you all right?" Harmony asked.

Boo leaned against his legs, lending strength, and Dale pulled himself together. "Peachy keen," he said dryly.

Harmony bit her lip. "Maybe we should just find a place to hole up and wait until dawn."

"What about fixing this thing? Resolving Wicklow's issues, burning his bones and all that?"

She shook her head slowly. "I'm pretty sure that Wicklow's bones are in the graveyard. Let's just lock ourselves in one of these rooms for a few hours. When it gets light out, we can figure out the next step."

"I thought you said that only one of us can leave when the sun rises."

He could see her mind working beneath those hazel eyes, but her features betrayed nothing. "That's purely conjecture on my part."

Dale wanted to object, but couldn't find the words to do so. Whatever was going on here, he had no idea how to deal with it. There was no procedure for this, no checklist or system. All his years of responding to emergencies didn't apply to this supernatural crisis.

"All right," he relented. "Let's find a place to hole up. Got any ideas?"

Harmony rolled her eyes. "What, you think because I've been haunting this place for six years I know where to hide from scary mist?"

"Well, do you?"

She hesitated, then said grudgingly, "Follow me."

She proceeded Dale and Boo down the hallway, around a corner and into another short corridor lined with doors. She stopped in front of one.

"What's in here?" Dale asked.

"I have no idea," Harmony said. "I just picked at random."

Now Dale rolled his eyes. "So, you don't really know the layout of this house?"

"I told you before that I have no memory of being here," she snorted. "Did you think I was making that up?"

"Of course not, I just… I'm kind of at sea, here, Harmony. Totally out of my depth." He gritted his teeth as he admitted, "I could really use some help."

"You're at sea, I'm at sea. We're out of our depth. We're both in the same boat: up a creek without a paddle." Her words started out desperately but ended with a giggle. "Who knew there were so many water-based metaphors for being totally screwed?"

He couldn't help but laugh along with her. "Okay, fine, so neither of us knows what we're doing. I guess we'll just have to go on instinct. And if your instinct led you to this door, then let's see what's on the other side."

"Let's hope those aren't famous last words," Harmony mumbled.

Dale reached out his hand, opened the door, and they crossed the threshold.

CHAPTER
TEN

Dale

On the other side, with the door closed behind them, Dale held his breath as he shone his flashlight around the pitch-black room and Harmony held the lantern aloft.

The room was empty.

"Okay," Harmony said. "That was a whole lot of build-up for nothing."

"Hey, at least it's quiet," Dale said. "And it doesn't smell like lemons."

"Touché," Harmony leaned against the wall, then slid down into a sitting position. Boo immediately curled up on her lap, overhanging in each direction. She rubbed his ears absently. "What's with that lemon smell, anyway? Did Wicklow love Pledge, or what?"

Dale shrugged and settled down next to her. Boo took advantage of the extra surface area, and stretched out across the two of them.

"You're the Wicklow expert," Dale said. "You tell me."

"I'm not an expert on anything," Harmony sighed. "I didn't even know that I was dead."

"You're not dead, you're just… not totally alive."

"Aw, thanks, buddy. I feel so much better now."

"Any time." Dale circled Boo's rope leash a few times around his hand, so the dog couldn't wander. The orange color gleamed bright in the dimness. Dale clicked off his flashlight. "Man, I'm beat."

"You and me both," she yawned.

He couldn't help but tease her. "How can a ghost be tired?"

"Don't ask me," she said. "I don't understand any of this."

Without thinking, he put an arm around her and pulled her close. In their shared laps, Boo snored lightly.

"We're in over our heads here," Dale murmured. Before she could reply, he added, "Another water metaphor, I know. You don't need to point it out."

She laughed tiredly and switched off the lantern. Darkness wrapped them, but it was cozy and comforting. Within a few minutes, all three of them were asleep.

"I'M SORRY."

Dale woke with a snap. The pleasant warmth created by Harmony and Boo was gone. He was alone and chilled to the bone. He groped for his flashlight and pressed the switch, but all that emerged was a flicker of yellow light. Automatically he glanced down for the orange cord which had linked him to Boo, but it was gone, too.

He pushed himself to his feet, squinting as he swung the weak strobe around. He had the sense that someone was with him, but he couldn't see who it was.

"Harmony? Boo?" He called their names quietly. After a moment, he added hesitatingly, "Aunt Kell?"

Lights flashed, red and blue, flickering off the surrounding trees. His cheek was wet. How had he gotten outside? Why was he lying in the grass?

"Dale," said a voice in his ear. "I'm so sorry."

He jerked, and found himself still seated on the floor. In the pale light that could only be coming from the electric lantern, Harmony was leaning over him, looking anxiously into his face. Dale glanced at his hand and saw the orange cord, and a moment later he saw Boo himself, peering over Harmony's shoulder.

"Was it a dream?" he asked groggily.

"I think so," Harmony said. "You were mumbling and moving around."

He shook his head sharply, then pressed finger and thumb to his eyes. "Man, that was weird. Seemed so real."

"Do you want to talk about it?"

Cold, in the wet grass. Alone but not alone.

"No." He stood abruptly. There was a reason he didn't talk about his past, about the people he had loved and lost. He just plowed through, moved onward, threw himself into whatever disaster might be waiting on his next call.

He closed his eyes and took a deep breath. Behind him, he heard Harmony rise to her feet. She laid a hand on his arm.

"I'm so sorry."

"You don't have to keep saying that," he snapped. He turned on her.

"Dale," she whispered. Her eyes were luminous.

He blustered on: "I mean, I appreciate it, but saying *I'm sorry* over and over again doesn't do a thing for me."

"Dale."

"What?"

"It wasn't me who said it."

"What?"

She gestured over his shoulder, and he turned back around.

The room, which had been dark and empty only a moment earlier, was beginning to show vague shapes and textures. The walls revealed themselves to be covered in a striated wallpaper that looked sticky to the touch. The floor, previously bare wood, was now a scuffed white tile. And in the middle of the room sat a shape, a vague outline of something he couldn't identify.

"What is that?" Dale asked in a low voice.

"I don't think it's a 'what.' I think it's a 'who,'" Harmony replied. She had become eerily calm. "And I think it's a 'who' that you know."

Of all the Whos in Whoville, Dale thought crazily, *why does this one belong to me?*

But he knew the answer. Even as he crept forward, toward the shape; even as it materialized slowly into the form of a woman huddled in a wheelchair, even as every cell in his body screamed at him to flee… all the while, he knew who this person was, and why she was here.

The shape in the wheelchair had its back toward the door. On the opposite wall, which had been blank when they'd entered the room, a window had formed. But it wasn't a bright window, overlooking a cheerful scene of the outdoors. It was grim, and dirty, looking out at a blank cinderblock wall.

"I'm sorry," the shape said. The voice, familiar and reviled, made his stomach clench. "I'm so sorry."

Harmony moved with him as Dale turned and beheld the woman he thought he had seen in the town hall the previous night. Her face was older, lined and misshapen by age, but it was undoubtedly her.

Dale whimpered, and hated the sound. It was small, and pitiful, and he didn't want to be either of those things. Especially not now.

"You know her?" Harmony asked.

"Aunt Kell," he sighed. "It's my aunt, Kell."

Harmony, reading the emotions on his face, said simply: "Tell me."

"It was *her* fault." His voice broke, and he drew in a ragged breath. Jeez, he sounded just like a little kid. He pulled himself together and tried again. "It was her fault that my family died. She was driving the minivan with all of us inside. It was raining, and she swerved for some reason. The van went off the road, and down a hill. She and I were the only ones who survived."

There. He'd done it spoken the words and now they were out in the world.

"I'm so sorry," Aunt Kell moaned.

"Yeah, that's what you always said," Dale replied harshly. "And I'll tell you now what I told you then: I don't care. I don't care how sorry you are. I don't care how much you hurt, or how much you miss your sister. I just *don't* care. You stole their lives, and you ruined mine. And I'm glad you're unhappy and tormented in a hole like this."

He leaned over and spoke directly to the apparition in front of him. "I hope that every breath you take is a misery."

Dale straightened and walked right out of the room, into the hallway, with Boo dragging along behind him. When they were both out of the room, Dale slammed the door behind him. He crumpled to the floor. Grief, dammed for years, overflowed his defenses. He began to cry, like the child he had been when his happiness had been stolen.

The next thing he knew, there was a cold nose in his face. He pulled the dog close. Then Harmony was beside him. She wrapped her arms around both of them and held on as Dale's breath hitched and his tears flowed.

"I can't save them," he grieved. "No matter what I do, they'll always be gone."

"I know," she whispered.

After a while, after a long while, Dale took a deep breath and sat up. He wiped his nose on his shirt.

"Wow. Can you believe how manly I am right now?"

Harmony smiled gently and fanned herself with her hand. "I do declare, you're giving me the vapors, sir," she said.

He laughed and ruffled Boo behind the ears. "So, that's what passes for a supernatural experience these days? Felt more like a bad episode of *Maury Povich*."

"Maury never did a bad episode, and you know it," Harmony snorted. "But then again, I've been lost in this house for half a decade, so what do I know?"

She peered at him from under her bangs, and he couldn't help but smile. She really had a way about her, did Harmony Lowell.

"Why would Wicklow make my aunt appear, anyway?" Dale asked. "Just to make me miserable? Just to show that he's inside my head?"

"I don't know that it has anything to do with Wicklow," Harmony mused. "It might just have been... well... you."

"What do you mean?"

"You're here, Dale. You're a part of this house now, just like I am. And whatever is inside you—inside your mind, inside your heart—is also part of this house."

"Oh, great," Dale said sarcastically. "That's really great news. Sounds like a fun time. Did you go through something like that when you first came here?"

"I don't—"

"Remember. Right." Dale shook his head. "Well, hiding out didn't turn out as well as we'd hoped. And even with everything that's happened, we're still no closer to figuring out how to get out of here."

"I'm sorry," Harmony said. "I wish I could be more help."

"You didn't cause this situation. It's not your fault."

It really wasn't, he knew that. But still, he had to bite down on frustration. Harmony had been here for years, and she really couldn't remember anything? If she could just get an inkling of what had happened when she'd first arrived, it might give them a leg up on this situation.

Something flickered in his mind. "Hey, do you have your camera? It was in the little room with your body, wasn't it?"

"It was." Harmony frowned. "And I can't believe I left it behind again."

"Don't worry about it." Dale said, "When you first came into the house, before you met Orrin, you were taking pictures, right?"

"Well, yeah."

"Maybe those pictures can tell us something."

"I guess it couldn't hurt," Harmony said slowly. "Although to be honest I'm not too thrilled about going back into that room."

"It's just a room," Dale said. "I don't think it's any more dangerous than the rest of this place."

"That's not saying much." She smiled thinly, and he smiled back.

"Good point," he replied. "I think it's our next best bet, though."

"You're right. I certainly don't have anything better to suggest."

Feeling energized, Dale rose to his feet and held out

his hand. Harmony ignored it and stood up on her own.

He eyed her. "Everything okay? I mean, aside from the obvious?"

She hesitated, then said, "I'm just wondering how many times I might have tried to do all this before, and yet I'm still stuck here."

"We can only do as much as we can do," Dale answered. "We're going to keep going for as long as we can, and try as many ways as we can think of to get out of here. There is an answer somewhere. It might be complicated, but it's out there."

"All answers are simple once you've figured them out," Harmony replied. "I guess I'm just not very optimistic that we'll figure this one out."

"I'll be optimistic for both of us," Dale said. "Okay?"

She nodded.

Dale switched on his flashlight and shone it around. The hallway seemed to stretch forever in both directions. Purple wallpaper, faded and stained in places, created a dizzying effect. "Um, not to retract my show of confidence, but do you happen to know where we are and how we get back to the main bedroom?"

Harmony turned on the electric lantern, peered down the hall, and said, "I think I can either get us there directly, or get us more lost."

"Well, let's get moving and see where we end up."

They spoke little as they traversed the corridors, with Boo ambling along beside them. Dale had been worried that Harmony might want to talk about that tear-jerking scene from earlier, but she kept mercifully quiet about it. And he was grateful for that. Over the years, he had tried to deal with his childhood trauma in a variety of ways, both traditional and nontraditional, and had eventually succeeded in bandaging his emotional wounds to the extent that he could function from day to day. The pain and anger were still there, obviously. But stirring all that up again now would be counterproductive, to say the least.

At last they found their way back to the wide balcony of the second floor, and from there they moved quickly through the double doors of the main bedroom, and into the cavernous sleeping chamber, with its canopy bed and the carved mantel. The fireplace was dark now, cold and black, as if a flame hadn't touched it in decades.

All of this Dale took in at a glance. Wasting no time, he started right into the closet. But Harmony didn't follow him. He came back out into the bedroom.

"What's wrong?" he asked, not trying to hide his impatience. He had no idea how long it had taken them to get here. His perception of time was off. It was the darkness that was doing it, being in those long hallways, with no way to see the outdoors. Even now, when he glanced at the windows, all he saw was a hazy blackness. There was no way to judge how much time had passed, or how many hours they had until sunrise.

"It's so strange," she said softly. "I don't know if I can go in there. That little room has been my coffin for the last six years. And now it's like we robbed my grave, and my body is lying down in the foyer, exposed to the elements." She shook her head. "I'm sorry. I know I sound crazy and that I'm wasting time."

Dale wanted to comfort her, but his impatience had sharpened into anxiety. Minutes were ticking away. "It's okay. You stay here; I'll get the camera."

He started toward the closet again, but Harmony said, "No, wait."

He turned back. "What?"

"There's something—I almost remembered something. But it's gone now."

He pursed his lips and prayed for calm. Then he walked her over to the fireplace and handed her Boo's leash. "You two stay here, okay? I'll be in and out in five seconds."

Something in his tone snapped the uncertainty out of her and brought her shoulders rigidly to square.

"Can you just wait one minute?" she flared. Wind slapped the window and sobbed in the chimney, as if in commiseration with her. Boo whined and backed away.

Harmony said, "I'm on the verge of remembering something, and it could be important. You know what happened last time we went into a room, the ghostly apparition and the emotional outburst. Maybe we can avoid something similar happening if you'll just stand still and let me think!"

He had wanted to argue right up until the words "ghostly apparition and emotional outburst." The idea of that happening again froze him in his tracks, and he stood obediently, still and silent.

"Thank you." She laid a hand on the fireplace, tracing the lines of the wood, caressing the delicately carved face in the mantel.

"I went in there willingly," she said at last. "I came up here to take pictures, and for some reason I walked, willingly and consciously, into that little room." She bit her lips in frustration. "It's just a snapshot of a memory. Feels like a warning, but I can't say for sure."

"So, what do we do, just leave the camera in there?" There was no way that Dale would let that happen. He needed to know.

"I don't know," Harmony replied. With uncertainty written on her every feature, she turned to the beautiful carved face on the mantelpiece. She looked at the carving long and hard. Finally, she whispered to it, "What do we do?"

The next instant, a fire flared to life in the hearth, and crackled vigorously, as if it had been expecting them. Boo yipped in surprise, and gave a tug on the leash which they both ignored. The wind, still gusting in the chimney, changed pitch and rattled out a sound which could only be a word.

"Live," it gasped, drawing out the short "i" in a long, rusty exhale. "*Liiiiive.*"

Harmony and Dale both gasped in shock. They looked at each other, wide-eyed. "Live?" Dale questioned. "That's her answer?"

Harmony opened her mouth to respond, then closed it again. Finally, she said, "I told you that all answers are simple."

He blew out an exasperated breath.

"Okay, great; so you're telling us that we should live," he said to the carving. "Thanks, head. Very helpful! We'll do our best."

He rounded on Harmony. "I'm going in there now.
You can come with me or stay here. But either way, I'm
going to get that camera."

Not giving her a chance to react, he gripped his
flashlight, whirled around and walked through the
closet, into the little antechamber. The camera was at
the foot of the cot, just as Dale remembered.

He picked it up, found the power button and
pressed it. Then he held his breath as he waited to see if
it would turn on. Given all the extraordinary things
that happened in this house, he hoped that a battery
staying charged for half a decade wasn't outside the
realm of possibility. But his heart sank as the screen
remained dark.

"There's a trick to it." Harmony said from the closet
doorway.

ELEVEN

Harmony

I s it weird to say that I felt more alive as I cradled that camera in my hands?

I still couldn't bring myself to enter the closet, never mind the little room behind it. So Dale came back out into the bedroom and handed the Canon over. As soon as he did, I caught a whiff of that special electronic odor that belongs to digital cameras, and every phantom cell in my phantom body flared to life.

"That camera smell," I sighed. "I can't believe how much I've missed it."

I held it out for Dale to enjoy, and, although his expression plainly said that he was humoring me, he inhaled deeply.

"Peculiar," he said. "But not unpleasant."

I pressed the power button, as Dale had done, but held it for a few extra seconds. After a brief lag, it powered on. The little machine was awake, battery indicator showing a full charge.

"Amazing that it's been lying in there for six years," I murmured. "It was a gift from my boyfriend."

Scott. All of a sudden, I remembered him, smiling and happy as he handed me the camera. It had been wrapped in jack-o'-lantern wrapping paper, topped with an orange bow. He had known me so well and had worked so hard to make me happy. But nothing had ever been enough.

"Wow, I am the worst," I said.

Dale murmured in disagreement, but I couldn't let myself off the hook.

"I've barely thought about Scott at all tonight." Grief and shame washed over me. "Even when I was alive, I took him for granted. I didn't really want to marry him, but I was too scared to let him go. I hope he's moved on and found someone to make him happy."

Obviously not wanting me to feel bad, Dale offered, "My aunt tried for years to get me to talk to her. Not even to forgive her, just to talk to her. And I've always refused, even though she's the only actual family I have left."

"Are you trying to make the point that both of us can be jerks sometimes?" I felt my lips curl ruefully.

"I'm saying that you're not the only one who can be insensitive about the people who are closest to you."

"Well, for what it's worth, I can't blame you for not wanting to speak to your aunt. What happened to your family was awful."

I could tell he didn't want to talk about it. But a

corner of his mouth lifted as he said, "Thanks, I guess."

I took a deep breath and looked him in the eye. "My former boyfriend's name is Scott Alderman. My parents are Marianne and Donald Lowell. My brothers are Peter and Frank. I want to go back to the world and see them all."

I gripped the camera lovingly. "And I want to take pictures again."

"You will." Dale spoke with determination. "I'll make sure of it."

The man was sweet, but he was missing the point. I said, "I appreciate that, Dale, I really do. But you don't have to save me. I'm going to save myself. And if you're very nice, maybe I'll save you too."

"Gee, thanks."

The sarcasm in his voice was welcome. I felt like we were both coming back to our old selves: walking, talking, and giving attitude.

"Okay, let's see what we've got here." I pushed some buttons, then tilted the camera so that we could both see the display. The screen flashed brightly. I winced with pain. "Whoa, sorry about that."

I fiddled with the controls while Dale blinked, trying to clear his vision.

"Alrighty, let's try this again," I said.

"Are you sure?" Dale asked. "Because I really don't have time for retinal surgery."

"Very funny."

Just in case, I closed my eyes before pushing the display switch again. When I opened them, an image of Wicklow House, seen through the iron gate, was lighting up the screen.

"Oh, nice shot." Dale leaned closer. "Is this the first picture you took here?"

"Yes. The camera has an auto-search feature, so I was able to queue up the pictures in the order that I took them."

"Fancy machine. And good thinking." Dale nodded. "Let's take the tour."

The next picture was Wicklow House from the driveway, with its many-gabled roofline sharply outlined against the sky.

"The violet hour," I murmured.

"What?" Dale asked.

"Remember I said that I wanted to get here during the magic hour? The pre-sunset light is called the violet hour. Usually, it's purplish and kind of mystical. But the sky was cloudy that day."

"Typical Halloween afternoon in this area," he said.

"Yes. I remember standing outside there, pointing the camera at the house. I remember it like it just happened." I closed my eyes again. "I was standing in the grass. It was covered with brown leaves. The air was damp and cold, but refreshing. Everything smelled like fall. I took this picture, and then in the next—"

My eyes popped open as I remembered something. "Oh my God. The next picture."

I clicked forward, and Dale leaned in. In the upper window, all the way to the right, was a gray shape. It looked human. And at the same time, it looked most emphatically *not* human.

"Whoa," he said.

"Right?"

The following picture showed two windows occupied. The one after that, three occupied windows. And so on and so on until all the windows in the front of the house were filled with figures, human and yet not.

"I remember this." A supernatural thrill shivered through me, as it had on the lawn that day. "I remember seeing the people in the windows. It was exhilarating and terrifying at the same time."

"You didn't want to run?"

"No. I know it's weird, but I felt like they were welcoming me. Like I'd come home. And I was also excited, because it seemed that I might actually get proof of life after death. If I'd known how much proof was actually coming, I probably wouldn't have been so enthusiastic."

I grasped for more memories, but they eluded me. "Next picture," I said.

There followed a sequence of shots, mostly unremarkable, of the inside of the house. The pictures began in the kitchen, then went to the dining room. Finally, we came to the library. And there, on the screen, in front of the fireplace, was another hazy figure. It stood as if with an elbow propped on the mantel. The shape was obviously human: the outline crisp, the form a silvery gray. I could almost make out features on the head-shaped blob at the top.

"Orrin," I breathed.

Dale looked from the screen to me, and back again. "Are you sure?"

I zoomed in on the image, thanking God for high

pixel content, until the hint of features was visible. Although this wasn't a photo of a living human visage, the facial characteristics were clear. It was the same face as the one in the painting on the staircase.

"Orrin Shulman," I marveled. "Hello again."

"Wow," Dale said. "I guess that proves… something."

Frustration welled, and I bit my lip. "Yes. But it's not going to get us out of here."

"Don't give up yet. Let's see the next pictures."

I continued to forward. The pictures were like a stop-motion capture of my journey through the house. Occasionally a shadowy figure could be seen in the background, and sometimes a sharp silhouette appeared. I assumed that these clearer forms were Orrin. He popped in and out like a pal who had tagged along on my photo excursion. And I supposed, in a way, that was exactly who he had been.

When my photographic travels through the house reached the foyer, Dale said, "Stop," and leaned closer to the camera.

"From the first minute I stepped into this house, I was fascinated by that floor," he told me. "And now I see why."

In that one image, the foyer floor glowed with an unearthly light. The white tiles were incandescent, with a moon-like luminosity. The black tiles seemed to swim, ink-like, with a dark life of their own.

"What do you think it is?" I asked.

Dale was staring fixedly at the enthralling image.

"I'm not sure," he replied at last. "Let's keep going."

We scrolled onward.

On the screen, Orrin and I moved up the stairs, across the landing, and into the master bedroom. There were some good close-ups of the carving on the mantelpiece, followed by a shot of Orrin standing by the closet. And then, at last, came a picture of the inside of the antechamber where my body had slumbered for more than half a decade.

In the picture, the room was so full of figures that the walls were almost invisible.

"I remember," I said faintly. "I got so freaked out from being in there. I didn't completely understand why I was so frightened, except that it was cold and pitch-black, and yet I could see everything. Suddenly I realized what time it was, and that the sun must have gone down. The last thing I wanted was to be in the house after dark, so I ran back out into the bedroom and—"

The picture on the camera started moving. Dale and I watched as the next few moments, the last of my life as it had been, unfolded before our eyes.

On the screen, I moved back into the bedroom, not far from the spot where we stood in the present time. I must have been taking pictures automatically, barely conscious of the movement of my finger. I left the main bedroom, moved down the wide hallway and stopped at the second-floor landing.

"Oh my God."

I wasn't even sure who had spoken, Dale or myself. I tried to say something more, but words failed me. I was hypnotized by what was unfolding on the screen.

"Harmony," Dale said tensely.

"I know," I murmured. We should go, we should run, we should find a safe place. But still I was spell-bound, watching my life end on the digital device in my hand.

In the bedroom, in the here and now, the fire in the fireplace roared to life again, bellowing up the chimney and blazing higher, fiercer than should have been possible.

Boo uttered a terrified bark and pulled sharply on the leash.

"Harmony," Dale repeated. "We have to go. Now."

I roused myself and looked around, panic finally biting through my daze. Through the double doors of the bedroom, a white-hot effulgence had begun to glow. Without another word, we raced down the short corridor and stood, as I had done six years earlier, on the landing, looking down at the foyer.

What we saw mirrored the display of the camera. My stomach dropped.

We were looking at a whirlpool of light. The foyer floor had twisted into a never-ending spiral, which was rotating, moving all points downward into a black hole. The suction from the energy created a vortex of wind. The walls of the foyer were crowded with unearthly, spectral apparitions. Their faces were blank, but I could feel their reality. As if they felt us, too, they looked up. In every phantom face, blue eyes burned. They were the same eyes we had seen earlier, when the mist had gathered in the foyer.

"Oh, no," Dale moaned. "No, no, no."

He swayed where he stood, and I had to grab him to

keep him from falling.

"What is it?" I cried. Despite all the scary things that had already happened tonight, I had never seen him so pale, so terrified. "What's wrong?"

His mouth worked as he summoned the strength to answer. Finally, he looked at me and said. "Those eyes. I know where I've seen them before."

CHAPTER
TWELVE

Dale

The world had turned upside down. Dale didn't understand what was happening. Panicked, he grabbed Harmony's hand and pulled her away from the railing, away from the roaring vortex and those accusing, ghostly gazes. Boo, obviously too rattled to object, moved with them.

"We have to run for it," Dale called, above the noise of the wind. "There's no way we'll make it through whatever is down there."

"No!" Harmony cried. She turned the camera so he could see it. "Watch."

On the screen, Harmony turned from the scene in the foyer and fled back into the bedroom, through the closet, and into the antechamber. The picture jostled as if the camera had been dropped. The screen went blank.

"I tried running before," Harmony yelled. "And we both tried hiding tonight. It won't work."

"So what do we do?"

Without a word, she lifted a hand and pointed toward the foyer. Dale shook his head, trying to deny what they both knew to be true. Six years earlier, Harmony had made the mistake of running, and she had become trapped there. The only chance they had of getting out was to go through.

Dale looked in her face and saw fear there. But he also saw determination.

"There's no guarantee this will work," he warned.

"There's no guarantee of anything, ever," she replied.

He nodded. "Okay."

Boo must have sensed their intention, because he barked sharply, pulling on his leash. Dale tried to grab him, to pick him up and carry him down the stairs. But the dog twisted, contorting himself. In a quick, deliberate motion, Boo ducked his head, and the collar slipped off his neck. He took off down the hallway.

"Boo!" Harmony cried.

She started to run after him, but Dale stopped her.

He had to shout to be heard over the turmoil. "He'll be okay!"

She turned terrified eyes his way. "How do you know?" she shouted back.

"Because he's smarter than both of us put together!"

Tears spilled from Harmony's eyes, but she nodded.

Dale stuffed Boo's collar in his pocket and sent up a prayer that they were making the right decision. Then he held out his hand.

Harmony paused long enough to sling her camera securely across her shoulders, and hook the lantern to a belt loop on her jeans. When that was done, she clasped his hand and gripped it firmly. They shared one last look to cement their resolve, and then they started down. Harmony, on the left, had her free hand on the wall. Dale's right hand held his flashlight; his wrist trailed the banister for guidance.

The foyer floor was completely obscured now, covered in churning mist. A cloud rose to meet them as they descended. Lightning flashed and wind roared. It was like walking into a tornado. Each step took them further into the maelstrom until it swallowed them up. After that, visuals were useless. They could only go on faith and feeling.

When Dale's wrist made contact with the newel post at the bottom of the stairs, he squeezed Harmony's fingers, and she stopped on the stair, next to him. They were only one step away from the foyer.

Dale gathered his strength and moved forward. Harmony moved with him and, as if of one mind, they took the last step together.

Remembering the twisting vortex of the floor tile, Dale half expected the floor to be moving, or gone altogether. But surprisingly, it held firm under their feet.

All around them, the storm still raged. And *rage*, Dale realized, was the correct term. They were standing in the midst of absolute fury. And there they were, small and exposed, vulnerable to whatever happened next.

Harmony shouted against the wind: "I don't know what to do except go to the center of the room. That seems to be where it's leading us."

Dale nodded and gripped her hand more tightly. "Are you ready?"

Wind whipped their hair, and lights flashed all around them.

"Not really," Harmony called back.

In spite of the situation, Dale grinned.

"Me neither," he shouted. "Let's do it."

Clothes rippling and eyes squinting against the wind, they inched their way toward the center of the room. As they moved, the tiles writhed and rotated, the spiral twisting its way into nothingness. For a moment, Dale thought they would be sucked down into some weird nether world. But they took one final step, and suddenly everything whirled to a stop.

Silence descended, thick as a blanket.

It was as if they had stepped into a vacuum. The air was still. The light was steady. But more than that...

"Harmony," Dale said in a low voice.

"Yeah," Harmony answered his unspoken question. "I don't think we're in Kansas anymore."

They were back in the main bedroom. But it was the bedroom as it must have been in another age. The wallpaper was fresh and bright; the floor was polished. A brocade canopy arched over the bed. Through the gleaming glass of the window, Dale glimpsed green grass and flowering trees.

"It's beautiful," Harmony murmured.

"It's a home," Dale replied simply.

There were three other people in the room, but they didn't seem to be aware of Harmony or Dale. The identity of two could only be guessed at, but the third was undoubtedly John William Wicklow, before time and tragedy had overtaken him.

The man in front of them wasn't a wrathful old codger. He was young and handsome, relaxed in an easy chair, smiling at the little boy on the floor who played with a train set. A pretty lady settled on the arm of the chair, leaned over and whispered something in the man's ear. He laughed and kissed the back of her hand.

Happy family.

Dale blinked, and the scene changed.

It was the same room, but the light had turned dark and forbidding. Happiness had fled. In the fireplace, a fire burned but was unable to combat the gloom. Rain pattered against the windowpane.

The little boy was huddled in the middle of the vast bed. His skin was pale, his hair lank against the pillow. There were circles under his eyes. A doctor bent over the bed, pressed a stethoscope to the boy's chest. A few feet away, Wicklow and his wife stood weeping, their arms around one another.

The doctor straightened and shook his head. The woman's legs gave way. Wicklow pulled her to her feet, but she pushed him away and steadied herself on the bed post.

Her lips moved as she spoke words, angry and accusing. Dale and Harmony couldn't hear, and yet they could. Her utterance whispered in the air all around them.

"There is only death in this house," she said.

"No." Wicklow pulled her to him and spoke with earnest anguish. "This house is full of life. I promise you, this house will *always* be full of life."

She pulled away and ran out the door.

Another blink, and the room was empty, the bed stripped, and the toys gone. The child's mother entered and turned in a slow circle as though surveying the desolation that had overtaken her life. She sank down on the bed, closed her eyes, and let herself fall backwards on the mattress. She extended her arms and gave herself up to whatever cruel fate would have her. As Dale and Harmony watched, she took two deep breaths, and that was all.

"She died of grief," Harmony marveled. "I didn't know that could really happen."

"Stress-related cardiomyopathy," Dale said automatically. "Broken heart syndrome. It's rare but not impossible."

A fraction of a second later, Wicklow rushed in, arms outstretched as if to catch what was already gone forever. He sagged against the bed post, devastated. Then he spoke.

"I promise," he said. "This house will always be full of life."

He turned and looked straight at them, as if he had known they were there all along. He started to walk closer, and everything went dark.

THIRTEEN

Dale

For a moment, the blackness was absolute and suffocating. Then the flashlight, still in Dale's hand, flicked to life, and their surroundings slowly became illuminated.

Dale thought he might say the same about himself. He, too, had slowly become illuminated.

He looked around, and found that they were in the library. He focused on the painting of Wicklow above the fireplace, and locked eyes with the man for whom he had a new understanding.

"This is all about family, isn't it?" he said softly.

Harmony hesitated, then answered slowly, "I guess you could say that."

Dale heard the uncertainty in her voice, but he ignored it and went on, speaking to Harmony and to Wicklow and to the house in general. "Human beings are built for love, aren't we? And when there's no one to share it, we're like an empty house: purposeless and lonely, waiting for our hearts to be filled."

He walked to the wall, paneled in wood that still stood rich and strong. He stroked it gently.

"What Wicklow went through, losing everyone. I know how that feels." He licked his lips and looked over at Harmony. "Can you blame him for not wanting to be alone? Or for holding on to that promise he made to his wife. Despite everything, despite even death?"

"But it's not just about keeping a promise, is it?" Harmony said acidly.

The tartness of her tone made Dale's lips turn up in amusement. He felt warm toward her, almost indulgent. His own eyes had been opened. Hers were still partly shut. "What do you mean?"

Harmony said, "Making a promise is a deliberate action: it's active, not reactive. But what Wicklow did wasn't about the honor of keeping a promise; it was just an instinctive reaction to his loss. Of course, their deaths were tragic, and I don't mean to minimize that. But whatever weird manipulation of physics has made this house inescapable, and however remarkable that might be, it's not honorable, and it's not admirable. It's just sad."

She still wasn't getting it.

Dale said, "But we're all capable of doing extreme things when we're desperate."

"What, you mean like running off to explore an abandoned house because you want to avoid your boyfriend?" Harmony laughed self-consciously.

"Hypothetically, yes." Dale remained serious. "Or swearing you'll never speak to your only surviving family member again."

She shrugged. "Yeah, okay. We're all equally guilty of doing extreme things. I mean, you and I haven't trapped anyone in a house for all eternity, but whatever. So, where does that leave us? What do we do now?"

Dale had been expecting that question. And he had an answer. The course of action was so clear to him, he wondered why he'd never thought of it before. "Upstairs in the bedroom, the carving on the mantel said to live. I think we should take her advice."

He held out his hand. Harmony studied it as if she didn't quite know what to make of it. Like she didn't want to be afraid, but she couldn't help being a little nervous.

"You're acting really weird," she blurted. "Is there something you're not telling me?"

Dale sighed and dropped his hand. "I don't know how to say this. It's going to sound kind of crazy."

"So what else is new?" She crossed her arms. "Tell me."

"Those figures in the foyer. Did you see their eyes?"

"Yes, they were blue and creepy. So what? A lot of things in the house are creepy, if not blue."

"They were my mother's eyes."

Harmony's mouth dropped open.

Quickly, she closed it again. Visibly striving for nonchalance, she said casually, "I apologize for the 'creepy' remark. How do you know they were your mother's eyes?"

"I remember them. From that night when my family was killed. She buckled me into the seatbelt, looked me in the eyes and smiled. Those eyes… they were the same as the ones that we both saw tonight."

"Wow." Harmony took a moment to digest this information. "What do you think that means?"

"It's what you said earlier. We're both a part of this house now. It—it shows us to ourselves, you know? And that's what it did, showed me my mother, the last time I saw her. I thought the eyes were menacing, but now I think they were just trying to tell me something."

"What do you think they were trying to tell you?"

He swallowed. "That I have to find a way to make up with Aunt Kell. I have to find a place within myself where I can—not forgive her, exactly, but love her in spite of what she did."

He waved his hand, summing up the entirety of their night together. "This trap we're in, it's made up of choices. We have to make the choice to live. Not just to be alive, but to live. Even if by living, we lose people we love."

"Or break the heart of someone we care about," Harmony murmured.

Dale nodded. "Exactly."

Harmony asked doubtfully, "So what are you thinking? That if we make the choice to live--really live-- then we can just walk right out of here?"

"I think so. I hope so."

"I'll be very irritated if it turns out to be that simple," she said.

"Someone once told me that all answers are basically simple," Dale teased.

"You know a lot of smart people." Harmony sighed, then shrugged. "Alright. Let's give it a go."

Together, they moved from the library into the living room, where Dale had dumped his gear when he first arrived. He wasn't surprised to see that it was gone now. It had all disappeared into the house like so many other things. But from upstairs, he was sure he heard the now-familiar click of Boo's toenails on the wooden floor.

The foyer had returned to its normal, quiet state. The pattern on the floor was unmoving. Harmony's body was still lying in blissful repose on the bench.

"What do we do about that thing?" Harmony asked.

"Don't worry. I'm pretty sure that when you walk out of here, it will join you."

They paused on the threshold, regarding the open door, and the square of night beyond it. The sky was still dark, but the darkness was fading, as if the nighttime itself was getting tired and losing color.

Dale murmured, "Can I say something bizarre?"

"Can I stop you?"

"This has been one of the best nights of my life."

Harmony rolled her eyes.

"It's true," he insisted. "I finally understand what it means to have a family, to have someone in your life that you want to give the world to."

He took both her hands in his. He kissed them, reverently, and lifted them to his cheeks. They felt soft and warm and very real.

"And that is my gift to you, Harmony Lowell. The world, and everything in it. This is your story now."

Without another word, Dale pushed Harmony out the door.

FOURTEEN

Harmony

T he next thing I knew, I was lying on the front lawn. My chest was on fire, and I was being crushed by an elephant. At least, that's what it felt like.

My eyes and mouth both popped open. All I saw was blackness. I groaned, grasping at my chest, willing my body to do its work and breathe. At last, I sucked in a long and terrible breath. My lungs inflated—my actual, physical lungs. The pain was almost as intense as the suffocation had been a moment earlier. I forced myself to exhale and inhale again, and then again.

Slowly, my chest cooled, and the elephant eased off and trundled away. My blood began to oxygenate, veins carried oxygen to my cells, and I realized that I was human once more. Human, and alive.

Dang, it hurt.

Little by little, my vision cleared, and I could see my own arm and hand, lying on brown grass. I moved my fingers, enjoying the flex of sinew and the feeling of the prickly grass against my fingertips. I was outside. I was out of the house.

I lifted my head slowly, perceiving the creak and strain of muscles which had not moved in over half a decade. As I'd suspected, I was on the front lawn of Wicklow House. Tentatively, I moved my eyes in the direction of the driveway. It was empty. Dale's car was gone.

That's when I remembered what had just happened. Dale. He had pushed me out the door. Had he followed me outside? Where was he?

I scrambled to my feet, but paid the price quickly, as pain shot through every nerve ending. I had to lean over, hands on knees, and take several more deep breaths.

Then I straightened and looked into the open front door of Wicklow House.

Dale stood on the other side. His eyes, those warm green eyes, were wide and sad. And yet, when he saw me, he smiled.

"Told you I would get you out," he said, somewhat smugly.

Grief and gratitude pierced my heart, but his words were enough to irritate me. Momentarily forgetting his situation, I stomped forward and stood at the foot of the porch stairs.

"You unbelievable idiot!" I exclaimed. "What do you think you're doing?"

"What I was meant to do," he replied calmly. "Saving you. I think I was born to save you. I think it's why I survived that car crash."

This was a big moment for Dale. I could see it in his face. He felt he'd discovered his life's true purpose. I opened my mouth to say something kind. Here's what came out: "That's very sweet, but also incredibly stupid. You don't have to save me, remember? I can save myself."

I looked at the facade of the house, at its cold, gray stone armor. There had to be a way to get him out. There just had to be. "And in this case, I think maybe I should save you, too," I added.

I thought back to what we had seen on my camera's screen: Orrin and I had gone into the closet, but apparently only I had come out. My body must have been trapped at that point. And Orrin—had he been free to leave? Was that why Dale had been able to push me out of the door?

"I want you to do something for me," Dale was saying from the other side of the doorway. "Harmony, are you listening?"

"Yes," I lied. I thought about Dale's body. Had it become trapped when we'd gone back in to get my camera?

"I want you to find my Aunt Kell." Dale's voice trembled with emotion as he outlined my final favor to him. "Find her and tell her that I forgive her."

That brought me up short. "But you haven't forgiven her. You told me that you were just going to try to love her. Are you asking me to lie?"

What if I went in through the kitchen, like I had before? Would I be able to go back out that way and take Dale with me?

He answered my question: "I'm asking you to put an old woman's mind to rest. Phrase it however you like, just go there and do this for me. Will you?"

I didn't bother responding. I was too busy trying to remember whether I had locked the kitchen window from the inside before.

Ugh. This was getting me nowhere. I looked up. The sky was still dark, but dawn was coming fast. Soon, Dale would fade to nothing, and he'd be trapped inside until who knew when. There was only one thing to do. I put my foot on the bottom stair.

"What do you think you're doing?" Dale asked.

The anxiety in his voice piqued my righteous feminine resolve. Any doubts that I'd been experiencing evaporated on the spot. Increasing my speed, I said, "I'm coming to get you."

I didn't give him time to reply. I simply walked up the porch stairs, straight through the open door and into his arms.

I don't think I planned to kiss him, but that's exactly what happened. And let me tell you, friends, that was one amazing kiss. Dale has quite a set of lips on him. And those firefighter arms… Well, you know.

Unfortunately, there wasn't a lot of time to enjoy it. I felt him begin to fade, felt his presence slowly begin to unmake itself around me.

I broke the kiss and took a deep, human, breath.

"Come on," I said. "We're not letting Wicklow get

away with this."

I grabbed for his hand, and missed. Or did I miss? Did my hand pass right through his? I decided not to pause to find out.

I marched out of the foyer and into the living room. Dale followed. The fireplace was cold and dark; Dale's gear was gone, absorbed back into the house. These were real, serious, ghostly doings. I didn't know the magic words or understand the physics behind the disappearance. All I knew, all I *had*, was the bone-deep understanding that if I gave up now, both of us would be lost. Maybe forever this time.

I continued through the living room and stormed into the library. Armed only with bravado, I stood in front of Wicklow's picture and called him out.

Now, don't get the idea that I'm some super-bad chick who never runs from a fight. In real life, in the day-to-day, I am proud to call myself a good old-fashioned fraidy-cat. But my blood was up. I was sick of this nonsense. And there was no way that Dale was going to take my place, just so he could feel all superior for the rest of eternity.

"John William Wicklow!" I thundered, just like I was in a movie. "Show yourself!"

And he did. Oh boy, did he ever.

Before I could blink, a wall of mist roared out of the painting. It swirled around me in a blinding rush. I was surrounded by that citrusy scent, but now it was the smell of lemons that had gone bad, fruit that was turning brown and mushy and rotten.

I whirled around to escape the odor and to avoid

being blinded. In front of me, the mist gathered, rose up, and took the shape of a ten-foot-tall Wicklow.

He opened his mouth and bellowed, but I stood my ground.

"Knock it off!" I snapped.

The bellowing broke off abruptly, and the mist stilled. Honest to God, it blinked like it was confused.

Dale had come up beside me. Like a specter in an old movie, he floated, now, instead of standing. I had to work fast.

To the manlike form in front of me, I said, "You're not John William Wicklow. You're just an echo of a decision that was made a long time ago. You don't have the power of life and death over me. Or Dale. Or anyone."

I turned to Dale. "See this mist? It's just a symbol. It's like the cheesiest metaphor that could ever be conceived in the mind of some hack writer. It's symbolism for feeling lost and alone. And the truth is, we're never really alone, and we're never really lost. All we have to do is reach out."

I extended my hand. Dale looked at it, not under-standing.

He said hesitantly, "Do you mean…"

"Come with me if you want to live," I joked. Then, more seriously, I restated: "If you want to live, come with me. Take my hand."

His eyes met mine.

I whispered, "Do you want to live, Dale?"

His lips pressed together, and his eyes darkened. I could practically see images of his life whizzing through his consciousness: the losses, the loneliness. And then, abruptly, he blinked. His jaw set.

"Yes," he said. "But I'll be very irritated if it turns out to be this simple."

I smiled, even as my eyes filled with tears. "Stop stealing my lines."

He reached out his pale, ghostly hand and clasped mine. As we touched, the realness of him came rushing back. I saw him take form and color. I heard him inhale a loud breath.

And then the floor dropped out from beneath us.

CHAPTER
FIFTEEN

Dale

A split-second later Dale was rolling on wet pavement, with Harmony rolling next to him. When their bodies stopped moving, Dale got slowly to his feet. He hadn't expected this turn of events, and he wasn't sure what to make of it.

He held out a hand to Harmony and pulled her into a standing position next to him. They were on a deserted road. It was night, the blacktop was wet, and the air smelled heavily of a recent rain. A single street-lamp cast faint light on the trees and the grassy embankment that bordered the road. Beyond the grass, trees rustled as damp wind gusted.

"Well," Harmony said slowly, "you said that you didn't want it to be simple."

Dale wanted to laugh, but he was too tired. "Careful what you wish for, right?"

"That's what they say." She turned in a circle, taking in their surroundings. "Any idea where we are?"

He shook his head. "Beats me. But at least we're out of that house."

"I'm not so sure about that," Harmony said.

He squinted at her. "Do you know something I don't?"

"Oh, tons of things. But nothing that really bears on this situation. I do have a feeling, though."

"What kind of feeling?" Dale was pretty sure he didn't want to know, but he couldn't stop himself from asking the question.

Before she could answer, they saw headlights in the distance. Dale moved automatically to the side of the road, and raised his arms, hoping to flag down a ride.

Harmony said, "You don't have to do that."

"Why not?"

She didn't answer, she just looked at him with eyes that were very wide, and suddenly very sad.

A moment later, he understood.

The vehicle reached them and passed on by. But as it did, Dale saw that his aunt was behind the wheel, and his father was in the front passenger seat. And he knew that behind the tinted windows of the rear seats were his mother, his sister, and his childhood self.

He managed to say, "Oh no," before the minivan's gravity grabbed him, and started pulling him along behind it.

"Harmony," he called desperately. He didn't know what was about to happen, but he didn't want to go through it alone. "Harmony!"

"I can't go with you," Harmony spoke softly, but he heard her loud and clear.

"Why not?" He was grabbing for her, frantically trying to stop himself from being pulled along with the car. He felt himself stretching as the car moved away, then he was skidding along behind it, and Harmony was getting smaller and smaller.

"I don't know," she called sadly. "I don't really understand any of this."

Dale felt a snap, and he was inside the car, in the back seat, squeezed in next to his childhood self. He was overwhelmed by the smells of the past: Cheerios and baby powder and a faint whiff of the cigarette his mother liked to sneak from time to time when she was driving by herself.

His sister Trina was in her car seat in the middle, playing with a stuffed animal, and Dale's mother was on the other side. She grinned at him as he whipped his head from one side to another.

He couldn't live through the accident again. He just couldn't. There had to be a way out of this situation.

"There's no way out," said his father's voice from the front passenger seat. Dale froze, wondering if they knew he was in the car with them. Then his father added, "No way except Route 23. That storm knocked down a lot of trees."

Dale heard an exasperated sigh, and from the front driver's seat spoke the woman he'd been avoiding for the past two decades.

"Fine," Aunt Kell said. "We'll take 23. But I bet the highway would be faster."

"And I bet everyone who's sitting in gridlock on that very highway thought the same thing," Dale's father groused.

"Hey now." His mother pushed lightly at her father's shoulder. "Don't be a grumpypants. We're celebrating tonight, remember?"

Celebrating? Dale thought, confused. He didn't remember that part of the story. What had they been—

"That's right. Our amazing son took first place in the science fair!" Dale's father peered over his shoulder.

Dale could see his own eyes, green and round, in his father's face. He groped for memory. Science fair? How had that been possible? He'd always been lousy at science. Hadn't he?

"Congratulations again, nephew," Aunt Kell sang.

He met her eyes in the rearview mirror, and she dropped him a wink.

"I'm proud of you, kid."

Dale's father spoke up again. "I'm proud of you, too."

In the back seat, his mother sighed loudly. "We're all equally proud of you, Dale."

In spite of himself, Dale smiled. He had forgotten this dynamic, where his father and his aunt pretended to dislike each other, and his mother played referee. It was silly, and maybe a little strange, but that was his family. Silly and strange.

And dead, of course. How could he forget that, even for a moment?

His smile faded.

Next to him, his little sister waggled her toy in his

117

childhood face. "Boo!" she said. "Boo!"

Wait, what?

Young Dale took the toy and held it up. "Blue," he enunciated. *"Blue."*

"Boo!" Trina crowed.

She snatched it back and chomped down on its plush blue snout. For the first time, Dale got a really good look at the stuffed animal. It was a dog, with a collar that jingled, and one ear that fell lopsided.

In the front seat, Kell chuckled. In an aside to Dale's father, she said, "Your kids are the greatest, you know that?"

Dale's father leaned his head back and smiled. "Yeah. I really do."

Dale's mother gave him a tender grin, reached over and ruffled his hair.

"Dale, one of these days, I'm going to get you a real dog," Aunt Kell chirped.

"Oh no you're not," Dale's father said.

"Oh yes, she is," Dale's mother chimed in. "And we'll name him Blue!"

"Boo!" Trina cried, laughing.

Dale, sitting next to his childhood self, closed his eyes. He remembered now. Remembered all of it. And he knew what came next.

He felt the car swerve, saw the headlights from the oncoming vehicle through his eyelids, heard the horn, heard the cries, felt the impact and the tumble-slide down the embankment. And through it all, he held on to that final exchange, that last good moment. Everything from that point forward would be grief, and pain, and weeping.

When Dale opened his eyes, he was lying in the wet grass, young and yet old, mourning for a loss he couldn't even fully grasp. He only knew that parts hurt, that everything was wrong.

The toy dog, looking very blue against the dark night, sat a few inches from his right hand. He grasped it, and pulled it toward him.

Harmony appeared in his field of vision. Her eyes were full of sadness. She said nothing, nor did she try to hold him. She merely lay down across from him, brought one hand up to her chest, as if she were clutching a plush toy of her own. The other hand stretched in his direction until their fingers met, and intertwined.

After a time, the police came, bringing ambulances and fire trucks. Lights flashed, red and blue, flickering off the surrounding trees. His cheek remained pressed against the grass, the dog clasped tightly against his chest.

"Dale," Aunt Kell's voice said in his ear. "I'm so sorry."

The world dropped away.

CHAPTER
SIXTEEN

Harmony

We fell.

The wet grass dissolved beneath our bodies, and then, somehow, we were tumbling through the sky, plummeting like dead weight. I was pretty sure that this would be the end.

Dale's hand was still firmly locked in mine. Our skin seemed fused together, and I had never been so glad to not be alone. He squeezed my fingers, and I looked over, squinting at him against the rush of frigid air. In his other hand, he still grasped his sister's little blue dog. At least the three of us were together at the end.

When our eyes met, Dale gave a rueful little smile, and a small shrug. The gesture seemed to say, *Oh, well. What are you gonna do?*

If I hadn't been so terrified, I would have laughed.

Below us, the earth spread out like a map. The delicate light of early morning revealed the rise and fall of hills and valleys, and etched toothpick-sized trees against the frozen earth. Wind whipped past us. In the east, a pink glow was visible along the horizon, as November dawned at last. Halloween was officially over.

The next thing I knew, the roof of Wicklow House appeared directly beneath us. We barely had time to brace ourselves before we punched through the slate shingles. There was a terrific crash. Dust and wood splinters flew everywhere. And still we continued to plummet, passing through the attic, breaking through to the second story.

Suddenly, we were in the secret room beyond the closet in the main bedroom. Dale's body was stretched out on the cot, as my own had been. Time slowed down. As we descended through the air, I saw Dale fall *into* his body and re-attach himself to it.

Then Dale and his body, me and mine, all fell together. We passed through the floor, spiders scurrying and dust exploding.

His hand slipped away from me, and I groped frantically, trying to find him in the chaos. At last, I found his fingers again. I grabbed on tight, and that was when we hit the floor.

CHAPTER

SEVENTEEN

Dale

Dale landed with a thud that rattled his teeth and knocked the wind clean out of him. His eyes were closed, but he felt, and heard, Harmony plop down on the floor next to him. He squeezed her fingers, and she squeezed back. Then they lay motionless for a moment, waiting to see what would happen next.

When nothing did happen, when all continued to be still and quiet around them, Dale opened his eyes. Above him, the ceiling was intact, which didn't make any sense, seeing as how they'd just fallen through it. On the other hand, none of this really made any sense, so what the heck?

Harmony groaned, "What a way to come back from the dead."

That made him laugh, which hurt like the devil.

They climbed to their feet, slowly, testing each phase of standing as they went.

Harmony looked down at her body, turning her palms upward and examining them like they were long-lost treasures. She spoke softly to her physical self. "I remember you. Thanks for hanging around for me."

Then she turned in a circle, gazing at the house. She put out a hand and touched Dale's arm lightly. "Do you see what I see?"

He looked around. He saw walls and windows, with sunlight coming in and pooling on the floor. From where he stood he could also see down the hall to the door of the kitchen, and into the living room, where the corner of his sleeping bag was visible.

"It's just a house," he said.

"Exactly," Harmony breathed. "It's just a house."

And it was.

Or at least, it seemed to be. The lemon smell was completely gone, and in its place hovered the scent of dust and old wood. Dale even thought he detected a hint of dampness, which in this case was encouraging.

"Do you think that Wicklow, or whatever that was, is gone?" Dale asked.

"I don't know," Harmony said slowly. "It's hard to believe that it would give up that easily. Could be that we just scared it away, or ticked it off enough that it let us go. Either way…"

"Either way, maybe we should get while the gettin' is good," Dale finished.

"Exactly."

They didn't stop to think, or to reflect on their experiences of the night before; they just moved as fast as they could.

It took them mere moments to gather up Dale's gear and load it back into his truck. Harmony's camera, still slung securely across her chest, winked in the sunlight. They found her car in the back, right where she'd always claimed it would be. Her keys were in the pocket of her jeans, her purse was in the trunk. The engine started right up when she turned the key. It wasn't until both cars were outside the gate that they finally stopped to look back at the house.

They stood, side by side, and gazed through the iron bars, down the drive, at Wicklow House. From this angle, it looked unchanged. But who could say? Its walls were keepers of secrets, its windows were blank eyes that revealed nothing. The only thing Dale knew for sure was that he was glad to be out.

"You know, if you hadn't come here last night, I would still be stuck in there," Harmony mused. "You really did save me. Thank you."

"Happy to return the favor." He flashed a smile. "You saved me, too, remember."

She hesitated, then asked, "Do you think you'll go see your aunt?"

"Yeah." He was a little surprised to hear the word come out of his mouth, but he was glad to hear it. "There were so many things about that night that I'd forgotten. The science fair, the funny relationship between my parents and my aunt, and…"

He trailed off, not sure how to bring up the dog. But

124

Harmony knew what he was thinking.

"Boo," she said for him. Her voice turned sad. "He didn't make it out with us, did he?"

Dale cleared his throat. He had wondered if she would notice, if she would even remember the phantom canine. "I don't think he was ever actually here. I think he was just some kind of manifestation of the house."

As if the universe wanted to make Dale eat his words, a happy bark exploded across the open air.

"Dale, look!" Harmony exclaimed.

In a second-floor window, Boo's face had appeared. He grinned at them through the glass, and barked again. Then he disappeared.

Harmony swung the gate open and started toward the house. After a moment, Dale followed.

"What are we doing?" he asked nervously. "Are we really going back into the haunted house to save the dog? Have we *never* seen a scary movie?"

"This isn't a movie, Dale," she said. "And I'm not scared. Are you?"

"No." And it was true, he wasn't. The house was just a house. And the past was in the past, where it should be. Whatever happened in the future, he knew he could face it.

At that moment, Boo exploded out of the front door, racing toward them in a joyous sprint. As if of one mind, he and Harmony knelt down and held out their arms. Boo bounded up to them, tail wagging and tongue licking, his whole body wriggling with joy.

Almost not wanting to ask the question, Dale spoke

hesitantly. "Do you think he's been real the whole time?"

"I think your love for him has always been real," Harmony replied. "And maybe we shouldn't look too far beyond that."

Dale nodded. It was true. Where Boo had come from wasn't really important. He was with them now, that was all that mattered. He remembered that he still had the dog's collar in his pocket. He pulled it out and fastened it around Boo's neck.

"Maybe he's been my dog all along," Dale mused.

Harmony grinned. "Told you."

Suddenly, she leapt to her feet. Then she threw her arms out and danced in a circle, looking up at the sky. "We're alive! Dale, we're alive!"

Looking at her blew the lid off the last of Dale's worry. Impulsively he stood, scooped her up and whirled her around. Boo frolicked at their feet.

"I'm going to eat the biggest breakfast ever!" Harmony crowed as she flew. "I haven't eaten in six years!"

He laughed and put her down. "And you're going to see your family?"

"First thing," she said. "Even before I eat."

"And what are you going to tell them?"

"The truth," she said. Then she smiled. "Or as much of it as they can handle without having me committed. I'll feel my way through it."

Her smile faded. "As for Scott, I'll have to figure that out when I see him. Like I said, I hope he's moved on and found someone to make him happy. Either way, I'll always be his friend."

Dale nodded. The ordeal that she had been through wasn't something that could be explained away or cleared up in a single conversation. He could see miles of questions and complications on the road in front of her. But personally, he thought that the happiness of her nearest and dearest would be so great it would eclipse everything else. At least for a time.

Harmony knelt back down and hugged Boo, then looked up at Dale. "How about you?" she asked. "What are you going to do?"

Speaking of happiness...

Dale dropped to his knees and cupped her face in his hands, relishing the realness of her, and the sight of her in the sunlight.

"I'm going to live," he said simply.

And he kissed her.

EPILOGUE

Harmony

And I guess this is where I leave you, Dear Reader. I do wish I could have told you in the beginning that everything came out okay, but that's not how storytelling works, as you probably know.

As for Wicklow House, I honestly don't know if anything—or any*one*—is still haunting it. I just know that it's not me. And for that, I am eternally grateful.

Dale locked the tall iron gate, then walked me to my car and opened the door for me. He closed it when I was inside and watched as I buckled my seat belt.

I rolled down the window, and he crouched next to the car.

"Do you remember how to get home?" he teased.

"Like I was just there yesterday," I answered smartly.

"And you have my number to call me later and let me know that everything is okay?"

"I do, indeed." I patted the pocket of my sweatshirt, where the piece of paper on which he'd written his phone number resided snugly.

"Good. Drive safe."

"You too."

He gave me a swift kiss, lingering not too long. Dale and I had agreed that I would have to talk to Scott before too much smooching could take place. But even the butterfly touch of his lips made my pulse gallop.

It was good to be alive.

Dale returned to his truck, where Boo waited patiently. When Dale opened the door, Boo hopped into the cab and moved into the passenger seat like he'd been doing it all his life. Maybe, in some sense, he had been.

Dale paused before climbing in. He cast one final look at the house. Then he looked at me and smiled. My heart turned over. He was quite a guy, that Firefighter Dale.

He got into the truck and closed the door. Through the back window, I saw him buckle his own seatbelt and reach over to ruffle Boo's ears.

Man and dog were off to find Dale's friend Jenner. Dale had offered to come with me to my parents' house, but I thought I should go alone. It would be enough of a shock to see me after all these years, never mind me showing up with a fella and a dog. And, again, there was Scott to consider.

Gentleman that Dale was, he waved for me to pull

out first. I obliged. He pulled onto the road after me, and in my rearview mirror I had the satisfaction of seeing him and Boo, riding right behind me.

I couldn't help but cast one final look over my shoulder before I rounded the corner that would take Wicklow House out of my sight. Maybe I'm wrong, but I thought I saw a pale, misty figure filling the window of the old main bedroom.

But it could have been my imagination. And either way, I didn't really care. I turned the corner and left the house behind me.

I checked my rearview again. Dale's mouth was moving, and I figured he was either singing or talking to Jenner on the speaker phone. Then I noticed that the dog was grinning at me.

My eyes met Boo's in the mirror.

Reader, I swear, he winked.

The End

AUTHOR'S NOTE

Hello again! You made it to the end. Yay! I hope that means that you enjoyed Dale and Harmony's romantic paranormal adventure. Please drop me a line and let me know what you thought. You can reach me at misha@mishacrews.com.

I actually wrote a draft of this story several years ago, but never finished it because I knew something was missing. Recently, as I was struggling to finish both the next book in my Angel River series, and my next romantic suspense novel, I decided that I wanted to try something completely different. So, I dusted off this old bauble and realized what the story lacked: a lovable mutt. That's how Boo became part of the story. I don't know how I ever conceived of it without him.

I have another "Halloweenish" story, called *All I Want for Christmas is a Happy Halloween*, which you can read for free when you sign up for my mailing list at this link. It's also available on Kindle if you'd rather get it that way.

Thank you as always for reading! I'll see you in the next book.

About the Author

Misha Crews is the bestselling author of multiple romantic novels and short stories. Readers have called her work "head and shoulders above the usual fare of contemporary romance novels," "absolutely fascinating," and "original." Born in Charlottesville, Virginia, Misha was raised near Washington, D.C., and now lives in the Shenandoah Valley, where she writes multiple genres of romance, mystery and adventure.

amazon.com/stores/author/B003ZNE5P0
facebook.com/MishaCrewsAuthor
instagram.com/mishacrews
goodreads.com/mishacrews
pinterest.com/MishaCrews

Also by Misha Crews

Angel River Novels

Homesong

The House on the Hill

The Book of Forgotten Angels

Sweet Music

Still Waters

One Secret Summer - coming 2025!

Romantic Suspense

Her Secret Bodyguard

To Keep Her Safe

Short Fiction

At the Cafe and Other Stories

The Magic Hour

The Violet Hour

All I Want for Christmas is a Happy Halloween

Printed in Dunstable, United Kingdom